CW00854302

Dead End in the Pyrenees

Dead End in the Pyrenees

Elly Grant

Books by the Author

Death in the Pyrenees series:

- Palm Trees in the Pyrenees

- Grass Grows in the Pyrenees

- Red Light in the Pyrenees

- Dead End in the Pyrenees

- Deadly Degrees in the Pyrenees

Angela Murphy series:

- The Unravelling of Thomas Malone

- The Coming of the Lord

Also by Elly Grant

- Never Ever Leave Me

- Death at Presley Park

- But Billy Can't Fly

- Twists and Turns

For my Friend Deborah Vass

Chapter 1

The blow to his head wasn't hard enough to render Monsieur Dupont unconscious, but it stupefied him. Blood poured profusely from a deep scalp wound, down into his left eye. He flopped onto the recently washed tiles at the side of the Roman bath, then floundered at the edge, frantically trying to stop his body from slipping completely into the pool. His upper torso overhung the edge, hands slapping at the water as he tried to right himself. He was aware of the metal chair, attached to a hoist to enable the disabled to enter the water, beginning to descend. As it lowered it trapped Monsieur Dupont, forcing his head and shoulders under the water. He struggled, his toes drumming the moist tiles, arms flapping uselessly, but he was hopelessly stuck. Soon he succumbed. Brimstone-smelling steam rose from the surface of the spa pool and silence returned.

When Madame Georges arrived for work, she was surprised to hear a low whirring sound coming from the pool area. She couldn't think what it might be. Surely the machinery and gadgets, designed to treat all manner of ailments, had been switched off at the close of business the night before? The last treatments were usually completed by 7pm, at which point everyone went home, leaving Monsieur Dupont, the caretaker, to lock up.

Following the sound, Madame Georges entered the majestic Roman spa. The double doors swung silently closed behind her as she made her way towards the pool. She was aware of her feet, still encased in outdoor shoes, making a slapping sound on the tiled floor. Madame Georges immediately noticed that the hoist chair was down and something was bundled up beneath it at the water's edge, but as her spectacles were steamed-up from the damp atmosphere, she couldn't tell what that something was until she was practically on top of it.

"Oh, mon Dieu!" she said aloud, on realising that what had appeared to be a bundle of rags, was in fact, a man.

A wave of shock passed through her body, and she took off her glasses with shaking hands, cleaned them on the hem of her blouse and stared again. It was definitely a man. His body was still and what seemed to be blood gathered in a puddle on the tiles beneath it. Madame Georges could not immediately recognise the person, as the head and shoulders were under water. All the staff at *les thermes* wore pink track-suits and trainers to work, and the guests were usually attired in white towelling, dressing gowns and blue rubber pool shoes. This person was clothed in a dark-coloured suit and had formal shoes on his feet.

Regaining some of her composure, Madame Georges turned and ran back through the double swing doors towards the office. She used her key to let herself in then immediately pressed the button to sound the alarm. The alarm was a wartime relic, a former air-raid siren, still used to alert people to an emergency. It wailed out over the valley and across the mountains twice. People who would normally have gone back to sleep at the first blast were now fully awake. The queue of chattering shoppers, waiting in line at the *boulangerie* to buy their baguettes fell silent, each person straining to listen for approaching emergency vehicles. This double call was used only for the most serious of incidents.

Madame Georges sank into a chair, then she picked up the phone to dial the emergency number and report what she'd discovered.

"Oh, mon Dieu, mon Dieu, a man is dead! I'm sure he is dead. There has been an accident, I think. Assistance, *s'il vous plait*, please come at once, please help me, I am alone here," she said, when the call was answered. Madame Georges had seen death before many times. The spa attracted the sick and the old searching for cures for various ailments, and many of them spent the last days of their lives there – but this was different.

Like a well-oiled machine, everything flowed into action. Before very long the *pompiers'* – who are both firemen and trained paramedics – arrived, along with an ambulance and a local practitioner named Doctor Poullet. A crowd began to gather in the street outside. But prior to this whole circus kicking off, I was the first on the scene, accompanied by one of my trainee officers. We managed to calm down Madame Georges before securing the area and this is where my story begins...

Chapter 2

Many of you will have met me before and know that I am a senior police officer living and working in the French side of the Eastern Pyrenees; but for everyone else, allow me to introduce myself. My name is Danielle and I am thirty-three years of age. Solving several serious crimes in my region has propelled my career forward at a very fast pace – especially quick for a woman – to the esteemed position I now enjoy. I oversee a large area, covering my small town and several nearby villages and farms. I have people working under me and I answer directly to my superior, Detective Gerard, who is based in Perpignan. My ambition is to have his job, but for the meantime, I have patience, I can wait.

I live with my best friend, Patricia, who is a lesbian. But don't make any incorrect assumptions please. She is like a sister to me. We do love each other, but there is no sexual side to our relationship. We have been friends since elementary school, where we were both treated as outsiders and shunned – she for being a tomboy and me for being dressed oddly by my strange and venomous mother.

Patricia and I reside in a beautiful house with our dog Ollee, and a lazy cat called Mimi. She treats us like hoteliers. Our home is situated on the edge of a village across the river from the town.

It is near enough for me to walk to work, should I wish to do so, but far enough away from the gossipers and the prying eyes.

Patricia produces pies and preserves, which she sells commercially. Her food is delicious and she has customers as far away as Paris. As well as this, she is a talented artist with her work being displayed and sold in several galleries. With Patricia's business and my job, we live very well. We are comfortable and have no money worries. You will learn more about my life and my friends, but for the meantime, let me tell you what is happening in the here and now.

I consider Doctor Poullet, who has just arrived at the spa, to be my friend. We have both attended the scenes of several crimes involving death and he has become the official medical examiner on call for the area. He is a cantankerous old devil, and he used to scare me with his sharp tongue and sarcastic quips, but I am used to him now, and more importantly, he is used to me.

"Ah, Danielle, bonjour," he says, unable to hide an annoyed scowl. "What a time to be called to this God-forsaken place. My wife had just put my coffee on the table. This room is like a sauna. Can nobody turn on some air conditioning? How can I be expected to work in these conditions?"

"Good morning, Doctor. I'm sorry, but this is a spa and spas are supposed to be warm and steamy. Just think how good it will be for our skin," I reply with a smirk. The doctor is always moaning about something, but he makes me laugh and I can't resist having a dig at him.

"Hmph," is his response. "Danielle, you are not funny. My shirt is stuck to my skin with sweat and I'm not getting any younger. What will you do if I have a stroke? Who will give you a report then?" His plump face is red and a river of perspiration is running down his forehead and dripping off his nose and chin. He loosens his tie and pulls at his collar, undoing the top button.

I back off. I forgot how irritated he gets early in the day. Doctor Poullet does not do mornings. With help from the *pompiers*, the chair is lifted and the body pulled onto the edge of the pool for the doctor to examine.

"He has been hit on the head, probably by the chair; there is a large gash, but I don't think that is what killed him. I think this man drowned. It is Monsieur Dupont, by the way," Poullet says.

"Dupont? The caretaker? Why is he dressed in a suit? Why was he here after hours?"

I turn in the direction of the male voice and see that Monsieur Claude, the owner of the spa, has arrived.

"Will one of you help me up?" Doctor Poullet snaps, struggling to lift his rotund frame from his squatting position beside the body. As my assistant endeavours to help him up, Poullet says, "If we knew all the answers, Claude, I could be enjoying my cup of coffee at home, Danielle could be taking a walk around town in the fresh air and Jean here," he nods towards the senior *pompier*, "Could be sitting on his arse, waiting for some idiot to set fire to something."

Claude visibly shrinks at the outburst, dropping his chin and staring at his feet.

"I'm sure this man drowned," Poullet continues. "It was probably an accident."

"I'm sorry to disagree, Poullet," Jean says, "but this equipment is unlikely to malfunction. I can't see how a person could accidentally hit their head on the chair, then switch on the mechanism to lower it. He might have been murdered. It needs investigating."

Poullet and I exchange glances. Monsieur Claude covers his face with his hands.

"Oh, mon Dieu, mon Dieu," Claude says. "This is the second unusual death in a week. Madame Carruthers, the English lady, came for her treatment, tripped on the stairs while entering the building and hit her head. She died immediately. We've only just completed the paperwork for that incident, and now this."

My old friend Jean turns to me. "You should inform your boss about this one, Danielle. I cannot agree that his death was accidental. I'm sorry, but the *pompiers* are responsible for checking that these machines are safe. All the spa equipment was given a clean bill of health, less than a month ago."

"It's true, I have the certificate," Claude adds.

"You people sort yourselves out," Poullet says. "I'm going home for my breakfast. You'll have my report on Monday, Danielle. I'm taking the weekend off, for a change." And without as much as an *au revoir*, the good doctor heaves his sweating form towards the exit. "Oh, and you can move the body now," he adds, without turning his head.

Jean and I exchange the usual pleasantries, asking kindly about each other's family and work as his men prepare the body for removal.

"I suppose you'll have to interview rather a lot of people. I apologise for causing you more work, but you do understand my position, don't you, Danielle?"

"Of course, Jean; of course I understand – but I still believe this could simply have been a terrible accident."

"Perhaps, perhaps," he concedes.

"I'm not sure what to do next," Monsieur Claude cuts in. "We'll have to empty the pool, there's blood in it." His mouth is puckered, as if there is a bad taste on his tongue. "That would normally be Monsieur Dupont's job. I'll have to call Albert in to do it now. And I'll have to cancel the 'curists', they'll be arriving for their treatments at any moment and my staff are all waiting outside."

"If I might suggest something," I say. "Why don't you set up a small table and chair at the entrance, and if Madame Georges is up to the task, have her sit there with one of my officers and turn people away as they arrive. She can note their names and explain what has happened. My officer can advise them that they may not leave town until we have their statements. The spa is due to close next week, for the winter break. You can shut down early and sort out the cleaning then."

Monsieur Claude purses his lips. "Yes, thank you Danielle. That makes a lot of sense. Most people have already finished their treatments by now. There are only a handful of them left completing their third week. Surely, I won't be expected to refund all their money when they've used our services and had most of the benefits by now? Perhaps I'll just return the fees for the final week or maybe I'll tell them to make a claim on their insurance. After all, why should I be out of pocket? It's bad enough that I'll be paying the staff for taking time off."

Jean and I exchange incredulous glances. A man is lying dead and all Claude can think about is how much money he will lose. He is one of the richest men in town, but one of the poorest when it comes to compassion, it seems. He scuttles off to find Madame Georges. Whatever her state of nerves, I'm sure she'll be pressed into working today.

Finally, Dupont's corpse is secured in a plastic body bag and loaded onto a trolley, then trundled through the door to the waiting ambulance. One wheel of the trolley is slightly wonky and the whole contraption squeaks and squeals as it is pushed along.

"That could do with being replaced," Jean says, nodding at the worn-out piece of equipment. "It's not very old, but obviously well-used."

"I'm afraid many people die here," I reply.

Jean gives a shudder, "Let's get out of here," he says. "For some reason this place always gives me the creeps."

Chapter 3

I now have the unenviable task of informing Bertrand Dupont's wife of his death. I've been told that she has been visiting her sister in Barcelona, but is due home at any time. They have one son, Emil, who lives and works in nearby Perpignan. With a heavy heart, I climb the hill behind the spa to the purpose-built apartments which sit in an elevated position above town. They are practically empty, as most of the visitors have now departed and only a very small number of these apartments are occupied all year round.

It is a cool, crisp morning and the bright sun dazzles me as I make my way. December is usually a dry month with clear, blue skies and lots of sunshine. Many visitors are returning to the north of the country, which is much wetter, and we are glad to see the back of them. It is a relief to have our town return to a slower pace of life as everyone and everything winds down and gets ready for the coming seasonal holidays.

I reach the building and take the lift. It vibrates alarmingly, so I make a mental note to descend using the stairs when I'm done. As the doors open at the fifth floor I see the hallway is in darkness. I search for a switch to activate the communal lighting, feeling my way along the corridor in the darkness and accidentally press the doorbell of an empty apartment. When I finally find the right button and the light comes on, I exhale my bated breath. It takes me only a moment to locate Dupont's apartment and I ring the bell. The door is immediately opened by a plump, middle-aged woman. Her dyed blonde hair is arranged in sausage-shaped curls and she is dressed all in black.

"Madame Dupont?" I speculate.

The woman shakes her head, stepping aside to usher me through the hallway and into a lounge. The room is full of large pieces of furniture, and the walls are lined with shelves stacked with an assortment of religious icons and ornaments. It is dismal and oppressive and reminds me of my mother's house. A rail-thin woman is sitting on the over-stuffed sofa. She constantly dabs at her eyes with a sodden handkerchief. It seems bad news travels fast and it's obvious she's already been informed of her husband's death. Still, I must advise her formally.

"I am very sorry, Madame, but I must inform you that we have found a body at the spa which has been identified as your husband, Bertrand Dupont."

Her shoulders heave with sobs as a wave of despair overcomes her. There is a moment of awkward silence.

"My name is Madame Da Silva," the plump woman says, breaking the tension. "I heard about Bertrand, so I met Collette when she got off the bus. It's a terrible business. How did the accident happen?"

"We do not know yet exactly how he met his death," I reply cautiously. "But it appears as if he may have drowned. We'll know more in a couple of days. In the meantime, I need Madame Dupont to formally identify the body – if she's up to it, of course."

Madame Dupont shuts her eyes and nods her head.

"I'll go with her," Madame Da Silva offers.

I am most grateful for her offer, as it saves me from having to hang around.

"Thank you, Madame," I say. "I'll send a car to collect you both and one of my officers will accompany you. Once again, I am very sorry for your loss Madame Dupont."

I turn to leave, anxious to get back into the fresh air.

"He told me there was a problem at work when I telephoned him from Barcelona yesterday. You don't think..." Madame Dupont cannot bring herself to finish the sentence.

"I am sure, Madame, he didn't take his own life," I reply, giving her the answer she needs to hear.

"Thank you, Officer," she replies, her voice little more than a whisper.

I take the opportunity to make my exit and race down the stairs and out of the building, before either woman has a chance to detain me further. It's such a relief to be back in the sunshine. As it's now nearly lunchtime, I return to my office, make a couple of calls, then pick up my car and drive towards home. I want to take some time out and talk to Patricia before I must face what is likely to be, a very busy afternoon.

When I pull up outside my house I'm surprised and disappointed to find Ollee doesn't hurtle down the garden to greet me. Patricia must be out and she's taken the dog with her, I suspect. I constructed a special dog flap in the door, to enable Ollee to come and go as he pleases when we're not at home and he always responds when he hears my car. Then I remember Patricia saying something this morning about meeting my father at the orchard. By this time of year, most of the pruning and tidying up is over, but they were planning on planting a couple of new fruit trees and I know they were due to be delivered sometime this week. I glance at my watch, decide to make myself some lunch, then stop at the orchard to say hello before I return to work. That way I get to eat and see my family for a few minutes as well.

Chapter 4

My office was always rather cramped, but recently, we've taken over the shop next door so we finally have space for every permanent member of staff to each have their own desk. The original tiny cloakroom with toilet is now for my personal use only, but a larger facility, which was part of the shop, may be used by all staff. When I emerge from my cloakroom after hanging up my coat, Paul, my most senior assistant officer, places a cup of steaming coffee on my desk.

"You're going to need this, Boss," he says. "The trainee you left at the spa has returned with a list of twenty-three names and he says more client's names may yet need to be added."

I groan. "Surely we don't need to interview them all? Hasn't he identified the people who had access to the pool area after the spa closed for the evening? I expected him to give me the names of the staff who have keys and the people whose treatment finished late in the day, not the entire list of 'curists' as well. Where is he now?"

"I sent him for lunch," Paul says. "Laurent has gone over to the spa to try and get the information we actually need. He's not the brightest bulb in the chandelier, but at least he knows the right questions to ask. You better sit down and have this with your coffee," he adds, placing an almond croissant beside the cup. "The sugar will give you strength."

I stare at him quizzically.

"I took the liberty, Boss," he explains. "I know how stressed you get when you have to speak to Detective Gerard and he's already been on the phone looking for you."

I groan again. "How on earth did he find out about this so quickly? Who told him?"

"Nobody, apparently – that is, not until he phoned looking for our monthly stats and Laurent let the cat out of the bag."

"I thought we emailed him that information two days ago?"

"Apparently not. Laurent accidentally emailed it to our own office instead of Gerard's."

"How is it that you and Laurent started here at the same time, yet you've advanced to being a cheeky smartass, while he's still marking time?"

Paul smiles and winks at me. "I don't know, Boss. Maybe it's because I'm a handsome devil and Laurent's a plod."

Maybe I'm being unfair, but I worked hard to get a permanent posting here for Paul because I rate his work so highly. Laurent, on the other hand, is slow on the uptake, but he's the son of an official in Perpignan and he was foisted on me.

I shake my head and rub my hand over my eyes. "You'd better get Gerard on the phone for me," I say. "But do me a favour and wait until after I've eaten my croissant."

I have no sooner finished my coffee when an angry Monsieur Claude arrives at the office. I can hear him shouting at Paul, so I go to investigate and when I open my door a very red-faced Claude turns on me.

"What right do the police have, going through my clients' and staffs' personal files?" he demands. "That information is very sensitive. Some of the employees of the spa are important medical personnel."

"You'd better come in to my office, Monsieur Claude. I'm not sure what you're talking about. My officer is simply seeking a list of key holders. Please, sit down and we'll try to get to the bottom of this."

He sits down, perching on the edge of the chair I offer, and I take my seat across from him.

"Now, let's start at the beginning," I say. "So far, only two of my officers have asked for information, Marcel, the trainee and Laurent, who you already know. Which one of them has been looking at the files?"

"No, Danielle, it wasn't one of them. It was the detective, the one in plain clothes. He had an official-looking letter giving him permission. He was in my office for over an hour, going through everything."

"I haven't sent anyone to your office," I reply with a frown. "Did you keep the letter he showed you?"

"No," he replies, "I thought it was okay. Are you telling me the man was a fraud? What on earth was he looking for?"

"I have absolutely no idea, Monsieur Claude. I was hoping you could tell me."

Claude looks sick. His colour has changed from bright red with anger to deathly white.

"I'd better get back to my office and see if anything is missing," he says, getting to his feet.

"Give a description of the man to Paul before you leave. I'll try to find out what I can," I offer. "If he's a stranger, one of my men might notice him in town because most of the 'curists' and tourists have left. In the meantime, please try to think about what he might have been searching for. I'm concerned that a stranger is snooping about, especially so soon after a suspicious death has occurred."

"Dupont drowned. It was an accident. Poullet will confirm that, I'm sure. There is nothing suspicious. Not in my pool and not in my files," Claude snaps before turning and storming out of my office, banging the door behind him.

I don't feel I can face speaking to Gerard at the moment so I send him an email instead, with the figures he's looking for together with a brief statement about the death of Dupont. I include an apology for not returning his phone call, making a lame excuse. I'm troubled that a member of my community has died in unusual circumstances and now someone is impersonating a policeman and poking around the place where he worked and was killed. This person has been very devious and determined. Something odd is going on and I plan to find out what it is.

Chapter 5

There is a thump on my bed and I wake with a start. It is a dark, still night. Suddenly, a wet nose and licking tongue is thrust under my chin. Ollee is snorting and snuffling and whimpering. Almost immediately, I hear a low rumble of thunder. It's clear that Patricia's bedroom door must be closed as she would be his first port of call in a storm. Ollee has never liked thunder. It always unsettles him and now he has unsettled me. I strain to listen but I don't hear any rain. It usually makes a rattling noise when it hits the metal roof of the shed. Maybe the storm will pass us by. Perhaps the rain will fall on the other side of the mountains; the Spanish side.

Ollee moves and makes himself comfortable, snuggled up to my legs. I push the dog away from me so that I can stretch out. He turns around and around a few times on the bedspread before once again plonking himself down, this time against my back. I have neither the strength nor the inclination to move him so I lie in the darkness with my eyes shut and attempt to drift off, but sleep eludes me.

I stare at the clock. It shows the time is 4.20am. Normally, on Saturday, I can sleep until late, but today is different. There is to be a Christmas market in the neighbouring town of Ceret and Patricia has been preparing for it for weeks. It will be a perfect platform for her to sell her preserves, which are beautifully packaged and designed to be given as gifts. All the jars are adorned with festive labels and are tied with bows and ribbons. Her profit margin is very high, because people pay more at Christmas. The venue will also enable her to do some marketing. Patricia has had flyers produced for her pies and preserves business. For her artwork, she has an album of photographs displaying paintings which are available for immediate purchase. There are always one or two people who leave the buying of gifts to the last minute. Usually they are English men, who are grateful for the opportunity of being able to buy a unique gift, whatever the cost. They're never short of money, but are often lazy and disorganised.

I know, in a mere two hours, I'll be expected to load up my car and drive us to the market. I'm tired, but my brain is too active to allow me to sleep. I keep thinking about what has taken place at the spa and, much as I'd prefer the death of Dupont to have been an accident, I cannot see how it could be.

The last time I remember looking at the clock, it showed 5.55. My alarm is ringing and I wake myself, but I'm still groggy. I must have finally dozed off but I've had only about half an hour's sleep. Ollee lifts his ears but he doesn't move as I struggle to get out of bed. I can hear Patricia, she's already awake and her singing is drifting upstairs from the kitchen below. When I emerge from the shower, I feel cooler but no less tired. Ollee pads downstairs at my heels.

"Bonjour mon ami," she says, smiling as I enter the kitchen. When I sit at the table she places a cup of coffee in front of me then turns to Ollee.

"Ah, mon petit, there you are, darling. I wondered where you'd got to when the thunder banged."

The dog wags his tail enthusiastically.

"He woke me up. Your door must have been shut," I accuse. I never wanted a dog in the first place and it is at times like this when I remember why.

"Oh, my poor baby," Paticia says, cooing at Ollee. He looks up at her with doleful eyes. "You were frightened and Mama's door was closed."

I sigh. It's clear I am relegated to second place behind the dog.

As we get ready to leave for the market, I'm pleased to see that today's supply of preserves are in uniform-sized jars and neatly packed into flat, cardboard boxes originally used to carry bananas, which makes them easy to handle. I load my Hyundai Tucson in no time at all, and with the back seats folded down, the precious cargo sits flat and secure. I marvel at all the little jars, labelled with enticing names like 'apricot conserve', 'fig chutney' and 'apple melange'. There are over two hundred jars, and with a profit margin of two euros each, it's a valuable load.

I admire Patricia immensely. From a bad start, orphaned at an early age, and with little help, she has become a very successful young woman. She would argue that without my input she'd still be working in her previous job at the local funeral parlour, and maybe that's true. Nevertheless, the transition from employee to business owner is huge and I'm so proud of her.

Once the car is fully loaded and the house locked up, Patricia, Ollee and I set off for Ceret. Patricia insists on playing an old CD of Christmas songs by the American singers Doris Day and Bing Crosby. "To get us in the mood," she says. For some reason, whenever she sings the words 'Jingle Bells', Ollee yips enthusiastically in accompaniment. It's a mad journey with us all squashed into the front seats and Ollee barking and Patricia singing and laughing and replaying 'Jingle Bells' over and over again, and although I'm still tired, it does lift my mood.

When we arrive at the market there is a buzz of excitement about the place, with a clanking of metal as stalls are constructed, voices chattering, bickering and instructing, all manner of goods being displayed, arranged and set out and children running around and playing together as their parents work. Adding to this hustle and bustle, a small flock of swifts fly back and forth above us, screeching as they feed on the wing. No doubt, once all the preparations are complete, everyone will hastily stuff themselves with croissants, or baguette and brie, washed down with steaming mugs of coffee to sustain them through the busy day ahead. There will be little time to eat again if the market is as busy as it is expected to be.

Setting up is easier for Patricia this morning, as her stall has already been constructed and put in place by Simon, the husband of Elodie, the *savonierre*. Elodie is a friend of ours from the dance class we attend. She lives in Ceret and she very kindly offered to store the stall for us after last month's market. Elodie also volunteered Simon's assistance to get it ready for today's sale.

Although the market is not due to begin for another hour, a queue, mostly made up of other vendors, is already forming at Patricia's stall. She begins to sell jars straight out of the cardboard boxes, and some people are buying four or six, and even ten at a time. I'm anxious to leave because I've ordered a special Christmas gift for Patricia from Elodie. I want to collect it and hide it in a box in the boot of my car so she doesn't see it, but I can't get away until this queue dissipates. Finally, after forty minutes of chaos and over two hundred and fifty euros worth of sales, I can leave.

"Take Ollee with you," Patricia says. "He's getting under my feet. Oh, and don't forget to buy the ham, and I nearly forgot, some crystallised ginger from Aude's stall, please."

I'm sure the list would have gone on and on, but for the arrival of a couple of English tourists looking at the photo album of paintings. So with Ollee jumping up and nipping at my sleeve, I make my escape.

It was a very cold start this morning. My breath froze in front of me as I worked and there was frost on the ground, but after the flurry of activity, I am too warm, so I unpeel my scarf and open my jacket. The sun has come up and the sky is clear blue.

The heady mix of scent emanating from Elodie's stall is intoxicating. A wonderful mix of fruit and flowers fills the air and I'm not surprised to see several people lifting and sniffing her soaps, trying to decide which of the pretty offerings to purchase. When she sees me Elodie immediately comes around to the front of the stall, leaving Simon to cope alone.

"Bonjour ma cheri," she says to Ollee, patting him on the head. "Bonjour Danielle." We exchange kisses on both cheeks. "I have the gift you ordered. Was the stall alright? Did Simon put it in the correct place?"

"Everything was perfect, thank you. Patricia has *un petit cadeau*, a little gift for Simon to thank him for his work. She'll give it to him herself, later. I didn't want Patricia to know I was coming over to see you, so I couldn't bring it with me."

"She didn't need to do that. Friends help each other. They don't expect rewards," Elodie replies, but I can see she is pleased by the gesture. "Simon loves Patricia's produce. I'm a terrible cook unless I'm making soap, then I always get the recipe right. Well, nearly always," she adds, laughing. "I'll just get your package now."

Elodie disappears around the back of her stall for a moment before returning with a large basket which is filled with a delightful confection. Little soaps shaped as oranges and lemons and scented with citrus; delicate rose, poppy and jasmine soaps, moulded to resemble the flowers they're perfumed with; miniature bee hive soaps smelling of honey; and little bottles of bubble bath, body lotion and moisturiser – it is a wonderful mixture and so pretty to the eye.

"Oh Elodie, it's beautiful! Patricia will love this gift. What do I owe you?" I ask, reaching for my wallet.

We argue over the price because she wants to give me too much of a discount, but we eventually agree on an amount and I take the lovely basket and hide it in the car. Then Ollee and I make our way to Monsieur Charles's stall, to buy the ham. After exchanging the usual greetings and pleasantries and with a large ham chosen and paid for, I am about to leave when Monsieur Charles takes my elbow and draws me to one side.

"Mind the stall for a minute," he instructs his assistant. "A moment of your time, Danielle," he says to me. "I want to talk to you about this business at the spa. Bertrand Dupont was a friend of mine. Or rather, his wife Collette was. We dated when we were younger," he says with a wink. "But still, I knew Bertrand quite well. We played pétanque together from time to time. I was in his company only last week and he was telling me about his concerns at work."

"What concerns did he have?" I ask. "Bertrand was the care-taker. Was he worried about some of the equipment, perhaps?"

"No, Danielle, nothing like that. He was concerned about the deaths at the spa. I know there are always people dying, par-ticularly in winter, and the spa attracts the old and the sick, but Bertrand told me that in the past two months, more than three times the usual number of deaths occurred. Seven people had died in two months. It bothered him. He's worked there for years. There has never been this number of deaths before." Monsieur Charles looks at the ground and kicks at a stone dis-tractedly with his toe. He's obviously finding it difficult to talk about this.

"I agree it is unusual," I reply. "But as you say, the spa attracts many people who are at the end of their lives and who are look-ing for a miracle to give them more time. It's probably just one of those things, just a glitch – but I'll keep an open mind when I'm doing my investigation. Thanks for letting me know and I'm sorry about your friend," I add.

Monsieur Charles gives a shrug and nods, then returns to the back of his stall. For a man who sells meat, he seems unusually uncomfortable discussing death, I think.

Ollee and I visit a few more stalls, buying delicacies as we go, then we return to Patricia who has practically sold out of her produce. She's also taken orders for three paintings which I'll have to deliver later in the day. Patricia has had a very successful and profitable sale and before very long we are heading for home. It is on the journey to our house that I begin to really consider what Monsieur Charles has told me. Dupont's wife also said he was troubled. Seven deaths in two months is a lot, I think. I must indeed investigate this further. Perhaps there's more to Dupont's demise than first meets the eye.

Chapter 6

Sunday morning heralds a flurry of to-ing and fro-ing and coming and going. The coffee pot is put on and is refilled throughout the day as all manner of produce and foodstuffs begin to fill our kitchen. Patricia is beaming.

"Look at all the things we have," she says happily, lovingly caressing each item as if it were made of gold.

Everything we could possibly want to eat during the holidays has miraculously appeared this morning in exchange for some of her preserves. There is a basket of nuts from Sophie, honey from Denis, a large duck from a local hunter whose name I don't know but who everyone calls 'Bang-Bang,' hand-made chocolates, flavoured coffee – the list goes on and on. Each item is delivered with conversation and camaraderie.

"Don't you just love this time of year?" Patricia asks and I nod and smile. "We'll have a full larder for Christmas and we won't have to spend one centime, everything will be bartered for."

The truth is that I hate having my space invaded by virtual strangers. I would much rather enjoy a quiet Sunday in the peace of my own home. I see enough people every day at work. But Patricia's working day is much more solitary, so I cannot deny her the joy she is feeling now. I keep out of her way and busy myself outside by seeing to our growing menagerie of chickens and rabbits. I mend something here and clear something there and pull up some weeds and dig the hard earth, and before very long the last visitor leaves and the busy day draws to an end.

We enjoy a delicious meal of *boeuf a la nicoise* which Patricia has prepared, washed down with rich, red wine and we are relaxing in front of the television when chaos ensues once again. Our cat suddenly appears and plonks herself down on the rug in front of the fire with a tiny kitten in her mouth. She proceeds to lovingly lick the fluffy bundle while holding it between her front paws.

"Oh Danielle, Danielle, is it dead?" Patricia cries, leaping to her feet. "I can't see it moving. Is it dead?"

Patricia worked in the local funeral parlour for years and was even able to apply make-up to enhance the look of corpses before burial, but for some reason, she is unable to handle the death of small creatures with the same detachment. I raise myself from my comfortable chair and on closer inspection I see the kitten move its head.

"It's alive," I state. "But it's very young. I think it still needs to be fed by its mother and our cat is definitely not its mother, because she's been spayed. I don't know where she's got it from."

"I'm calling Sarah, she'll know what to do," Patricia replies, and before I can say anything else, she's on the phone arranging for her to come around. Sarah is the local expert on all things meowing or barking. So much for my quiet evening in front of the television, I think.

Sarah duly arrives and both she and Patricia fuss and coo over the tiny bundle. Ollee tries to add his input to the proceedings by sticking his wet nose where it's not wanted and he's promptly banished to his bed. He stares miserably, head on paws, sighing dejectedly from time to time, but remains in his place. I know exactly how he feels. After two hours, Sarah finally leaves and Patricia has instructions about how to care for the kitten.

"Sarah says it's a boy," Patricia says. "Maybe I'll call him Gabriel after the angel because he's so angelic, or Noel, because it will soon be Christmas. He's a little gift from God," she adds and stares pointedly at me, challenging me to disagree.

"Why not just call him Jesus and be done with it," I say sarcastically.

"That's perfect, Danielle!" she replies. "We'll call you Jesus," she says to the little cat pronouncing the name in the Spanish manner – 'Hey-sus'.

I shake my head. "I give up," I mutter.

I leave Patricia and the cats and take Ollee for his evening walk. I'm not sure which one of us is happier to be out of the house. For once, I'm actually looking forward to getting back to work on Monday morning.

Chapter 7

Mid-morning on Monday I receive an email from Detective Gerard. It is a one-liner, simply acknowledging receipt of the one I sent him. There is no specific mention of Dupont, no words of encouragement or offers of help, but that seems to be par for the course now and I suppose I prefer it that way. It's good to feel trusted and in control, but in moments of self-doubt I can also feel left out on a limb. Patricia telephones me for the second time to report on Mimi our cat and her new 'son', Jesus. She also informs me that Clara, one of our hens, has produced the biggest egg she has ever seen. Who names a creature which will someday be cooked in a pot for soup? I have to ask her not to phone again, unless it is an emergency and then I feel guilty because I know she's frightened that her tiny charge may die and she'll have to cope alone if he does.

Marcel arrives back in the office. He had been sent to sort out a parking problem. There are often parking problems, even in winter, because people are selfish and lazy and would rather cause an obstruction than walk ten metres to the bank or the post office. Marcel has a man with him who he is gripping by the elbow. The man's face is red and he appears to be angry – fuming in fact – but he's not saying anything.

"This is the so-called 'detective'," Marcel says, unable to hide his delight. "I found him asking questions at the café, so I apprehended him."

I observe his captive. He is short and slim with a comb-over hairstyle and a pencil-thin moustache. His eyes are narrow and his lips are thin. He looks shifty, more like a villain than a detective.

Finally, the man speaks. "On what charge? On what charge have you brought me here? I am a detective. I have my I.D. in my pocket. If you'd let go of my arm, I can show you," he splutters.

"You'd better come into my office and we'll sort this out," I say. I glare at Marcel. He shrinks under my gaze and releases the man's arm.

When everyone has calmed down and we are seated in my office drinking coffee, the man, whose name is Gregory Armand, produces his identity papers and then explains why he's in town.

"As you can see, I am a private detective," he says, pocketing his I.D. papers. "I've been hired by Monsieur Daniel Falandry," he begins, "to investigate the death of his wife and the disposal of her estate. She died here in this town; at the spa, in fact. Her death was reported to be caused by a heart attack and maybe it was," he adds.

"Is there perhaps some doubt?" I ask. "Surely the death certificate will have recorded the cause of death?"

He hesitates and takes a sip of his coffee.

"I'd better start at the beginning," he says. "Madame and Monsieur Falandry have been estranged for over forty years, but they never divorced because of their religious beliefs. She returned to her mother's house when they separated and that's the property in question. Naturally, Falandry thought the house would pass directly to him if she died first as they had no children, but that was not the case. It seems the house was transferred to a Monsieur Claude shortly before her death. Monsieur Falandry wants to know why it is now in the possession of the owner of the spa where his wife died, particularly as no money seems to have changed hands."

"Maybe she didn't want her husband to have it? You said yourself they'd been separated for a long time. Perhaps she exchanged it as payment for years of treatment at the spa. Who paid for her funeral?" I ask. The truth is, I don't understand how this came about either. The circumstances are very odd.

"Well, there's the thing," Armand says. "Falandry was sent a copy of the bill for the funeral which had been paid for by the spa, together with a few personal effects which had been held in a bank – otherwise he wouldn't have known about her death."

"So what do you propose to do?" I ask.

"There is nothing I can do," he replies miserably. "Monsieur Claude is refusing to speak to me and he won't allow me to enter the spa again or speak to his staff.

"Can you blame him?" I ask. "You did trick your way into his office and you went through his files. I'm surprised he's not trying to press some sort of charge on you."

Armand smiles sheepishly. "It was a bit cheeky, granted, but Claude was the beneficiary of the gift. I thought he might have something to hide and maybe he has. It does all seem rather strange, doesn't it?"

"What are your plans then? Are you returning to... where did you say you are from?"

"Beziers, I'm returning to Beziers, but not just yet. First, I want to talk to the doctor who signed the death certificate. I saw from the records at the spa that Marie Falandry had terminal cancer, yet she died from a heart attack. I want to know what occurred on the day she died. I must return with some information, or I won't get my fee. Falandry is a mean and greedy man. He lives with, and supports a woman half his age."

"He should be pleased to be rid of his wife then," I say. "He'll be free to re-marry now."

"Pah, he doesn't want to re-marry. Why should he when he can have his cake and eat it? He just wants his wife's estate. He just wanted the house so he could sell it. It's the money he's after." He sips his coffee again. "Do you know the name of the doctor who signed the death certificate?" he asks, changing the subject. "I didn't get a note of it. Was it a local man?"

"I'm sorry, I can't help you there," I reply. "It might have been someone from out of town."

I can't meet his stare and I'm sure he knows I am lying, but he doesn't press the matter. I rise from my chair and so does Armand. I'm ending this meeting now, before he has the opportunity of asking me something else that I won't wish to answer. I intend to speak to Doctor Poullet myself, as I too want to know what happened to Madame Falandry.

The day passes quickly and when I next look at the clock it is two-thirty and I haven't yet had lunch, so leaving the office in Paul's capable hands, I make my escape and head for the cafe. I'm delighted to see my friend Byron sitting at a table by the entrance. His long, lean frame is elegantly clad, his coat unmistakably Armani. He sucks on a slim panatela while seemingly deep in thought. For the past six weeks, he's been in England sorting out a family problem and I was beginning to think he wouldn't return until after the New Year began. I don't have time for most of the English who have settled here, I find them crass and ignorant, but Byron is the exception to the rule.

"Bonjour, Byron, ça va?" I say as I approach.

He glances up. "Danielle, my darling girl," he says standing. "Will you join me?"

"Thank you, yes," I reply leaning towards him to give and receive the customary kisses. "I'm famished. I haven't had lunch yet, so I hope I'm not too late to get a sandwich."

"I'll just go and see, shall I?" he says, and being the perfect gentleman, Byron disappears inside to give my order. Within a few minutes, a cup of coffee and a baguette stuffed with ham and cheese is placed in front of me.

"Well now, what's been happening while I've been away?" he asks. "Have you missed me?"

"You have no idea how much," I reply honestly.

I hadn't realised just how much time I spent in Byron's company, sharing a coffee here or a sandwich there. I don't have many friends and most of the ones I do have are women. Byron is an older man, probably nearer to my father's age than mine. He is handsome, wealthy and educated and our friendship has developed over the past couple of years. I trust him to behave like a gentleman and not spoil our relationship by making a pass at me and he has never let me down. I value Byron's advice and I know he can keep a secret and will never reveal a confidence.

"Dupont from the spa has been killed. Drowned, we think. Poullet will probably send me the report before the day is out. It might even be on my desk by now," I inform him.

"Yes, someone told me about that. Terrible business; was it an accident?"

I shrug. "Not sure," I say. "Time will tell, no doubt."

Byron starts to talk about his family problem in England. The subject is obviously weighing heavily on his mind.

"It was my elderly aunt," he says. "She's got dementia and it's serious. She's gone completely ga-ga, I'm afraid. She doesn't even remember her own name. It's so sad. She was a college professor, you know. Now she's reduced to this state."

"I'm really sorry, Byron," I say sincerely. "Are you close?"

"Yes, very – she is my mother's only sister and she was good fun. I used to spend my school holidays with her every year when I was young. It's been an absolute bugger finding a care home to take her, in her current condition. There are very few places willing and able to handle someone like my aunt with kindness and patience. The best of them have waiting lists."

"Is there no family to look after her? Has she no children?"

"She has one daughter, my cousin Jenny, but it would be impossible for her to cope. Aunt Jill is too far gone," he replies. "Part of the problem is the cost of long-term care. If Aunt Jill owned nothing, the state would pay, but because she owns a house, she has to pay until her funds run out. That's why I was in the UK. I had to help Jenny to sell her mum's house as quickly as possible. With the current state of the economy the market's not good, but we managed, thank God."

"So, because your aunt was prudent the state can steal your cousin's inheritance? That's terrible," I say.

"I agree, it's very unfair – if she'd squandered her money the care would be free, but as it is, she has to pay nearly seven hundred pounds per week."

I'm completely shocked. What he has said makes me begin to think about my mother and father and I wonder what I would do if faced with the same dilemma. I think perhaps it is something I should discuss with a lawyer, in case a problem arises. I would care for my father in a heartbeat, but my mother is a different story. We have never got on and I wouldn't spend a single moment in her company that I didn't have to.

I was going to tell Byron about Madame Falandry and the detective, but given our previous conversation, I think better of it.

Chapter 8

When I return to work, I see Doctor Poullet is sitting in the outer office. His round face is shiny with perspiration, in spite of the air-conditioning, and he constantly mops it with a linen handkerchief.

"Bonjour, Poullet – are you waiting to see me?" I ask.

"What a great job you have, enjoying your lunch until nearly 4.30 when others are working from dawn until dusk," he replies. "I just thought I'd rest a while in these salubrious surroundings and perhaps engage with your sophisticated staff."

He stares pointedly at Laurent, who is attempting to excavate something from his nostril with the index finger of his left hand. Poullet rolls his eyes. Paul, who is sitting at a desk alongside tries, but fails, to stifle a guffaw.

"You'd better come in to my office," I say. I don't explain my late lunch. It's none of his business, besides, I am mildly annoyed.

Before I get a chance to offer he says, "I won't have coffee, just water and none of that rubbish out of the tap, some of the bottled stuff you keep in your fridge, please."

I smile to myself. The bottle in the fridge has been filled from the tap, it is simply chilling, but I make a point of letting him see me pour it nevertheless. Pompous old fool, I think. I am about to ask him why he's here when he slaps a large, brown envelope onto my desk.

"Bashed on the head then died from drowning, just as I suspected. His lungs were full of spa water. I've spoken to Jean, the chief *pompier*, and he confirms the equipment was in perfect working order. I now believe Dupont might have been murdered and so does Jean."

I am unhappy with this result, people die in accidents all the time, but murder is unsettling. It will upset the whole community. Everyone will have an opinion and they will all suspect each other.

"Merde," I say. "That's all I need."

Poullet nods in agreement.

"While you're here my friend, I have to tell you that a man from Beziers is looking for you. At least, he's looking for the doctor who signed a particular death certificate."

I notice a flash of concern pass over Poullet's face. His expression lasts for a split second, but I see it.

"I know some people who live in Bezier," he says, his previous demeanour returning. "Should I be familiar with this man?"

"I don't think so. He's a detective and he's investigating the death of a lady called Marie Falandry."

"Ah, the widow Falandry. She died of a heart attack. No relatives. Nice woman. Had a lot of pain from cancer and was beginning to lose her dignity, poor soul. I respected her and I liked her, she'd had a hard life, being widowed so young."

"I'm sorry for anyone with her health problems," I say. "But what makes you think she was a widow? She was estranged from her husband, but he is very much alive and it is he who has sent the detective."

I watch Poullet. His face pales and as he lifts his glass to his lips to gulp down some water, I see his hand is shaking.

"Marie told Claude that she had no family," Poullet replies. "What does this man want?"

"It's something to do with her estate, I think. Something about her mother's house."

"I see, I see." Poullet noticeably relaxes. "She died of a heart attack, it was very quick," he stresses. "I was there when she died, so there was no need for a post-mortem. Her death was witnessed you see, so there will be no problem in winding up her estate. If you see the detective again, please give him my number and I'll talk to him, then he can return to Beziers and be out of our hair."

"It's not that simple, my friend. It seems that before she died, she transferred her home to Monsieur Claude. It was worth quite a sizeable sum and her husband wants the money."

"What? What? Claude has her money, you say? I don't believe it. Why would he have inherited her estate?"

"No Poullet, the house was transferred before her death. Several months before, I think."

"Oh, I see, I see," he says. But his pale, sickly expression tells me he does not see at all.

"I have to go," he says heaving his rotund frame out of the chair. "Some of us must work. It'll be time for your coffee break now, I suppose. Or perhaps another trip to the cafe or to a bar, or maybe home for an early finish?" he adds with a wry smile.

He cannot forgive my late lunch it seems, or perhaps he's simply trying to cover his discomfort regarding Madame Falandry.

I try to speak to Monsieur Claude at the spa before close of day, but when I arrive I'm informed by Madame Georges that he left with Poullet ten minutes before. I guess he'll know all there is to know now. I hope Claude has a good story prepared, because although he can avoid speaking to the detective, he can't avoid me.

Chapter 9

Tuesday is usually my day off, but with the spectre of murder and the possibility of corruption hanging over the town, there will be no breaks until everyone concerned has been questioned. As it is normally quiet at this time of year, my officers expect extra time off, not less and they are lethargic and miserable, but it can't be helped.

"Patricia is on the phone," Paul calls from the outer office. "She wants to know if you'll be home early enough to drive her to Perpignan."

"Merde," I mutter. I forgot she was planning to visit the gallery. Two of her paintings have been sold and she wants to collect her money.

"You'd better put her through," I reply.

I brace myself for recriminations, but after the usual update on the menagerie, she assures me there's no problem.

"Marjorie's offered to drive me," she explains.

Marjorie is the wife of our esteemed Mayor and has proved herself to be a good friend.

"She's going to pick up her husband's new suit and she would like my company. We'll have lunch by the canal, then we intend to try the outdoor ice-rink that's been set up as part of the Christmas market. As usual, it will be very small and the blades on their skates are often blunt, but I can take my own skates and I'm sure the exercise will do me good. I'm leaving Ollee at home, but don't worry about him, he'll be fine."

The dog is the last thing on my mind at this moment. The truth is, I'm rather jealous. I would much prefer to be skating in Perpignan than interviewing potential murder suspects and it sounds as if Patricia would much rather spend the day having fun with Marjorie than with me. After we say our goodbyes, I have Paul track down Monsieur Claude and make arrangements for me to speak to him. This is not an easy task, because Claude has gone into hiding and seems to be trying to avoid me, but the sooner I begin the interviews, the sooner they'll be over.

* * *

"Bonjour, bonjour," Claude says, greeting me like an old friend and shaking my hand enthusiastically. "I've been hoping to have a chat with you," he adds.

"You have?" I ask sceptically.

"Oh yes, of course, yes – we must get this horrible business cleared up before I start taking bookings for the new season. We need to assure people that a terrible accident such as this will never happen again."

I'm accompanied by Laurent, who stares at me incredulously.

"Monsieur Claude," I say. "I think we'd better sit down. According to the reports I've received, both the doctor and the *pompiers* think we're dealing with a murder, not an accident."

Claude sits down heavily on his chair. "Oh, mon Dieu. How can that be? Who would want to murder Dupont?" He looks sick. "Am I now at risk? Could the murderer come after me next... or indeed, any of my staff?" he adds as an afterthought.

I hadn't considered Claude to be a potential victim. I saw him more as a suspect, but what if it's the spa that's being targeted and not the individual? This throws a whole new light on things.

In fact, Claude's reaction reduces the suspicion I feel towards him.

"I assure you, Monsieur Claude, the police will stop at nothing until this matter is resolved, but remember there's still a slim chance that no-one is involved and an accident actually occurred."

"A very, very slim chance," Laurent adds and I glower at him.

He turns his face away and nibbles on a fingernail.

"Idiot," I mutter. "Could someone have mistaken Dupont for you because he was wearing a suit?" I ask Claude.

"It's possible, but unlikely," Claude replies. "Everyone knows me and besides, Dupont and I have a different build, so even if the light was subdued, which it can be in the pool area, it would be obvious he wasn't me. Do you think someone meant to kill me but got poor Dupont instead?" Claude looks shocked and I don't blame him. He shifts uncomfortably in his chair.

"Perhaps, but at this stage I just don't know. We have to cover every possibility."

"But who would want to kill me? I've never hurt a soul in my life. I endeavour to improve people's lives, not harm them."

My mind immediately returns to Madame Falandry and the detective sent to investigate her death, but I decide to keep that thought to myself for now. "Were you the last to leave the spa on the evening in question?" I ask.

"Let me see," Claude begins. "All the office staff went home. They tend to leave right on the button. Dupont said he wanted to see me about something, but when I looked for him, Albert told me he'd already left. Albert was just finishing up. From my office, I heard him shout *au revoir* and the front door bang shut. Ten minutes later, I too left and I locked up behind me."

"Could Dupont have re-entered the building as Albert left?"

"I suppose so, but he didn't come to the office. Why would he enter the pool area dressed in his suit? And why was he dressed in his suit? I've only ever seen him wear one in church or at funerals."

"I guess he was dressed for a funeral. His own," Laurent quips and I glower at him again. This is no time for bad jokes. He returns to gnawing on his fingernails.

"And there was definitely no-one else in the building? All the staff and the clients were gone. You were the last person to leave?"

"I can't swear to it, but I think that was the case. Maybe Dupont returned later and had an accident after all, because I certainly didn't kill him. I didn't even know he was here. He was one of the key holders," he stresses.

"That wouldn't explain the reason Dupont was in the building after hours," I say. "I think we'll leave it at that for now, Monsieur Claude. I'll need to speak to Albert, but I'd like to meet with you later in the week to discuss another matter. Shall we say three o'clock on Thursday?"

Claude is deathly pale. There is no question that he knows what I want to discuss.

"Do you want to meet here?"

"I think that would be appropriate," I reply. "Don't you?"

"Until then," he says resignedly. He doesn't rise from his seat, and as there is nobody else in the building for us to question currently, Laurent and I see ourselves out.

Chapter 10

Unable to speak to Albert because he has an appointment at the *notaire*, I fulfil Poullet's prophesy and leave for home a bit early. Albert will keep until tomorrow, because there's plenty of time as the week looms long.

The scent of home-made apple pie reaches me as I approach the front door and my nostrils are assaulted by the delicious aroma of hot sugar, cinnamon and the acidic tartness of cooked apple when I enter the house. Patricia and Marjorie are sitting at the kitchen table, laughing. With their encouragement, Ollee is trying to retrieve his ball which has rolled beside Mimi and Jesus, but every time the dog approaches the cats, Mimi hisses and hits out a paw with claws extended. He jumps back, barking. Patricia and Marjorie clap their hands with delight.

"Bravo, you brave boy," Marjorie calls.

"Go on, Ollee, get your ball," Patricia says, and the frustrated creature tries again with the same result.

"You two are bad, cruel women," I say as I step over, lift the ball and give it to the dog. He immediately runs out of the door with it.

"You're early," Patricia says. "I thought you'd be later, but dinner is ready any time you want it."

"I'd better go," Marjorie says and she stands to leave.

"Sit down, sit down," I reply. "It's early, not nearly time for dinner, but if you wouldn't mind pouring me a cup of coffee, Patricia, and cutting me a piece of that pie, I'll join you for a chat. How are things with you, Marjorie? Is the family well?"

"Yes, yes, everything is good. My brother, Gilbert, is coming to visit on Friday, just for the weekend. He's bringing his friend Stuart with him."

Marjorie adores her younger brother, but she hardly ever gets to see him, and as far as I know, he never visits here. She always travels to him. Gilbert is the black sheep of her family, not for any wrongdoing, but simply because he's gay, and whilst everyone claims to have a gay acquaintance, nobody would admit to having such a person as a relative. I think her brother's preference was the reason Marjorie befriended Patricia so readily in the first place and having acceptance from the wife of the Mayor meant that our living arrangement was more easily tolerated. Whilst only a handful of people call us friend, most either ignore us or respect us, and although Patricia and I have a purely platonic relationship, many people probably assume otherwise.

"Will they be staying with you?" I ask.

Marjorie bites her lip and looks at Patricia; her eyes fill with tears and I think she may cry.

"Marjorie doesn't have the room without disrupting the children," Patricia states. "I thought they might stay here. They could have my room and we could double up. It's just for two nights. What do you think?"

I hate being put on the spot, but I guess it's my own fault for asking the question. Patricia didn't really have the chance to broach the subject with me on my own and I suppose it might be considered inappropriate for Gilbert to share a room with his partner when there are children in the house.

"Of course they'll stay here," I reply. By the determined look on Patricia's face, she's already decided, so why rock the boat? It's only for two nights, I reason. "It will be good to have company. I just hope they don't mind sharing their bed with a dog, because whilst they might be able to move Patricia out of her room, Ollee is an entirely different matter."

Patricia beams at me and Marjorie promptly bursts into tears.

"I don't know how to thank you," she sobs. "I didn't know what to do. Francis flatly refused to have them stay at our house, because with him being the Mayor, people come to call all the time and you know how folk talk. But how can I deny my brother hospitality? I rarely get to see him, and besides, he said he's got something important to discuss with me."

"They're arriving at lunch time," Patricia informs me. "I'll make dinner here for us all on Friday evening. Do you think your husband and the children will come?" she asks Marjorie.

"My husband will, but I'll leave the children at home. I don't know what Gilbert wants to discuss and perhaps it's something they shouldn't hear."

We sit in silence for a moment.

"I've just remembered we've got tickets for the charity dance at the Community Centre on Saturday night. I'm assuming you'll be going as well," I say to Marjorie. "We'd better get another couple of tickets, Patricia. It looks like you and I will have hot dates. That should certainly get tongues wagging."

"Bless you, Danielle. Bless you both," Marjorie says. "You are true friends and I can't thank you enough for your kindness. Now, if you'll excuse me, I really had better get going or my family will be hungry tonight, because unlike you, Patricia, my dinner is not yet prepared."

After Marjorie leaves I go upstairs to have a quick shower and get changed, leaving Patricia to organise dinner. From the outside our house looks like a small cottage but when you are inside it is like Dr. Who's TARDIS and is surprisingly spacious, although we seem to fill every inch of it. Apart from one instance when Patricia invited a date to spend the night – an incident we do not speak of – no one has ever shared our home. I feel quite apprehensive about strangers staying here, but we're committed now.

"What do you know about Gilbert and Stuart?" I ask when we are seated at the table.

"Not much, except of course that our esteemed Mayor won't have them stay in his home. Marjorie thinks he's homophobic, but I think he's just scared of the unknown. Francis has always been okay with me, but then, I'm not related to him."

"Does Gilbert still live in Paris?"

"At the moment, yes. They met and lived together in Scotland, in Stuart's home town of Glasgow, then they spent time in London and in Paris, but Marjorie thinks they're planning to return to live in Glasgow permanently. She thinks that's one of the things Gilbert wants to discuss."

"Francis should be pleased about that," I suggest. "Out of sight, out of mind."

"You're not upset about them staying here, are you, Danielle? You don't think I've made a mistake by offering, do you?"

I look at Patricia's worried face and my heart melts. Her kindness and unconditional generosity of spirit are two of the qualities that make me love her.

"No, darling, you did absolutely the right thing in offering," I say. "Just so long as you don't steal the duvet or kick me in your sleep. And, by the way, I'm not sharing my bed with Ollee; the dog sleeps somewhere else."

At the mention of his name, Ollee lifts his head and gives a small yip. Patricia and the dog exchange glances.

"There, there, baby," she says in a placatory fashion.

"At this rate, I'll be in the dog's bed and he'll be in mine," I protest.

"Don't be silly," Patricia says, laughing. "Ollee knows his place."

So she says, but I'm not sure, I'm not sure at all.

Chapter 11

In the morning, I telephone Madame Georges to arrange a meeting. As she was the person who found Monsieur Dupont's body, it's important that I question her further. I have her original statement, but there's little to go on and I need all the help I can get. She wants to meet at the spa and explains that although the last of the 'curists' sessions have been cancelled and most of the staff given garden leave, she has a mountain of paperwork to get through before she can close things down for the winter break.

"When you come to my office the door will be locked. I'm not taking any chances of a murderer creeping up on me while I'm working," she explains. "If you knock and call out so I know who you are, I'll let you in."

It dawns on me just how frightened and wary people are. I arrange the interview for eleven o'clock and at twelve, I'm meeting Jean and a couple of his men at the pool. Today we'll attempt to establish whether Dupont could have had an accident and if it was physically possible for him to hit his head then set the hoist in motion. I hope to speak to Albert, the assistant caretaker, in the afternoon. It's going to be a busy day and I won't have time to pop home for lunch. Patricia's apprehension about the impending arrival of Gilbert and Stuart has changed to excitement and she is manically tidying and cleaning the house so I'm not unhappy to be busy and out of her hair.

At precisely eleven, I knock on the office door.

"Madame Georges, it is Danielle." I hear a faint scurrying then silence. I knock again. "Madame Georges, it is Danielle. I'm here for our appointment."

Almost immediately a lock is turned, I hear a bolt being pulled and the door is opened. Madame Georges peers out at me. Her hair is askew, clumps of it sticking out from her head at crazy angles, as if she's been scratching her fingers through it. In her hand, she wields a large stapler, holding it like a weapon in front of her and her eyes hold the startled look of a deer caught in the headlights.

"Come in, sit down," she says and she drags a chair over to her desk for me. Madame Georges scurries around and sits in her chair, peering at me defensively, the desk creating a barrier between us.

"I've already given a statement to the police," she says. "I don't know what else I can say."

"Sometimes we remember things after the shock has passed. Why don't we talk about Monsieur Dupont? Did you notice anything unusual about him on the days before he died? Do you remember him saying or doing anything that struck you as odd? Or did he have any disagreements with anyone; perhaps another member of staff?"

"Well, everyone knew that he and Albert didn't really get on. Bertrand Dupont was very straight-laced, he took his job seriously. He moaned about the pay, of course, but everybody does. Albert drinks, you see. Often, he came to work late, sometimes hungover and occasionally still drunk. Bertrand would get very annoyed. Albert thought Bertrand was a buffoon, he mimicked him and made fun of him."

"Do you think Albert had a grudge against Monsieur Dupont?"

"No, definitely not. He didn't take him seriously enough."

"How can Albert afford to be drunk so often?" I ask. "I remember his parents were killed a couple of years ago, when their car crashed on the way to St. John. His father was drunk then – maybe alcoholism runs in his family. An assistant caretaker can't earn very much and by the time he pays for rent and food, surely there's nothing much left?"

"You're right about his parents, but Albert doesn't pay rent. He lives in a studio apartment in a block managed by his cousin, Michelle. His father used to own the building, along with a large house situated on the street behind the *boulangeire*, but when he died Michelle took possession of the buildings. She had some paperwork lodged at the *notaire* which showed Albert's father owed her money. But between you and I," Madame Georges says conspiratorially, "I think Michelle was in cahoots with Monsieur Boutiere the *notaire* and between them, they stole Albert's inheritance. I think there have been a few dodgy dealings between our estate agent and our *notaire*. Michelle Moliner is not liked and Pascal Boutiere is not trusted. Everyone knows Michelle cheats the English who come here to buy, but nobody cares about them. Anyway, she allows Albert to live in the apartment building rent free, the building which rightfully should have been his. She does this in exchange for some maintenance work. He's very bitter about it."

Madame Georges promptly shuts up. She looks down at her desk, picks up a pen and begins to doodle on a scrap of paper. Perhaps she thinks she's said too much and it doesn't seem as if she'll tell me any more today. After a few moments of silence, she finally looks up.

"Will that be all? Can you excuse me?" she asks. "I've much to do."

"Yes, yes, of course," I say. "But I may need to speak to you again," I add.

She stands, drops her chin and chews at her bottom lip. "As you wish," she says.

* * *

At times like this, Jean especially enjoys having the job of Chief *Pompier*. It means he can stand under the air-conditioning unit and give instructions, while his men, stripped down to T-shirts and shorts are kneeling and stretching, reaching and crawling in the steamy heat of the spa pool. I stand beside Jean as we choreograph every scenario, however improbable, with the hoist. From time to time, I see Albert skulking in the shadows of the periphery so I know he's turned up for our meeting. Finally, we discover one possible way in which Dupont could have hit his head then grabbed for the hoist, successfully pressing the button to lower the chair – but this event is highly unlikely. He would have had to reach through the bars of the equipment then pull his arm back as the chair lowered. And for him to then become trapped between the pool edge and the seat, he would have needed to lie down, overhanging the edge in exactly the right place.

"I must concede, Danielle, an accident is possible, but most unlikely," Jean says. "Dupont would have had more chance of winning the lottery than experiencing all the circumstances required to die in that manner. I'm now – more than ever before – sure he was murdered. I think someone swung the chair around on purpose and caught Dupont at the side of the head with the safety bar." Jean demonstrates, using one of his men as the hapless victim. "As he stumbled to the floor," he continues, "Dupont could perhaps have been overhanging the edge, making it easy for the same person to activate and lower the chair trapping him under it."

As I watch, I see that the fireman used in the demonstration might have suffered the same fate as Dupont had there not been two other men standing by to save him.

"That's a very convincing picture you've painted, Jean," I say, as the poor man is dragged spluttering from the water. And I'm sorry to admit that it looks as if I am indeed seeking a murderer, although at this stage I cannot rule out an accident, however unlikely. "Will you send me your findings in writing, please?"

"Of course," Jean replies. "I'll email it to you tomorrow if that's okay. By the way, are you and Patricia going to the charity event on Saturday? I'm taking a table with some friends if you want to join us."

I thank him for inviting me and explain that we will be there, but we expect to be joining Marjorie and her family.

"Her brother Gilbert and his friend will be coming with us," I explain.

"Is this the brother who lives in Paris," Jean asks. "The one nobody dares speak about because he's gay?"

"That's right," I reply. "And you mustn't say anything either," I warn. "Marjorie is our dear friend and as far as anyone will be concerned Gilbert and Stuart are guests of Patricia and me."

Jean begins to chuckle, "And which two of your party will be wearing the dresses?" he asks.

"I'm warning you Jean," I say, slapping him on the arm then waggling my pointed finger at him, but I cannot help laughing, nevertheless. I'm a bit concerned, however, about the reaction of others. The conversation between Jean and I is that of trusted friends, whereas strangers might not be so forgiving. Our party's behaviour at this event must be exemplary.

I leave Jean and his men and go in search of Albert, who now seems to have left the pool area. I walk through the swing doors and make my way down a long, narrow corridor which leads to the storerooms, activating a switch – which is on a timer – to light my way. Before I am halfway down the narrow passage I'm plunged into darkness. I look around, searching for another switch which should be illuminated, but there is no sign of one, and the area is pitch black. In a blind panic, I feel around the wall beside me for the button. My hand touches someone else's in the darkness before the light suddenly comes on. With my heart pounding in my chest, I realise that I'm standing practically toe-to-toe with Albert, who looms over me.

"We must have both reached for the switch at the same time," he suggests with a sneer. "I hope you weren't afraid of the dark."

I say nothing. My heart is still pounding and my mouth is dry. I'm sure he's lying. He must have been waiting in one of the storerooms for the lights to go out, then he simply stepped forward and covered the switch with his hand so I couldn't see it. I believe he wanted to scare me and he certainly succeeded.

"Thank you for coming in for our meeting," I say, finally finding my voice. "Is there somewhere we can sit and talk?"

"Please come into my office," he replies, pushing open a door beside him to reveal a small, windowless space. The room holds mops, buckets, deck scrubbers and the likes. At the end, there is a tiny coffee table and two plastic garden chairs. With the added bulk of Albert, the space feels claustrophobic.

"Do sit down," he says. "Make yourself comfortable. Coffee?"

He chuckles to himself as if he's told a joke and my instinct is to run. I feel trapped, the room is airless. I'm sweating and the walls seem to be closing in on me. Albert is grinning.

"It's not quite as smart as Monsieur Claude's, is it? But I don't suppose he'd let us use his luxurious office with its polished wooden, leather-topped desk and its window overlooking the square. This cupboard is all I'm worth, it seems," he adds bitterly.

"Why don't we just go for a walk and talk, Albert," I suggest. "Neither of us has to be here any longer today. We could sit by the river."

"Or we can go to the cafe for a pastis," he replies with a wink. "I'm sure I'll remember much more when I'm relaxed."

"Seat by the river first, cafe later, perhaps," I offer. I've noticed he's already slurring his words and I can smell a sour, stale aroma from his skin and clothes. He's obviously had a bucketful of alcohol last night and more today; another drink and he'll be of no use to me.

"Okay, Officer," he concedes. "You're the boss."

But I don't think he believes that for a minute. I think Albert is a controlling bully. He's probably been made to feel inferior all his life and this is the way he reacts when he's put on the spot. I'll have to be careful how I question him and selective in what I believe from his answers.

As we make our way towards the riverside I purposely take the route past Michelle Moliner's estate agency.

"This is your cousin's place, isn't it? She's done well for herself. She's a very clever woman," I add, baiting him.

"You might think she's clever," Albert replies. "But I know she's really a monster. Michelle has lied and cheated all her life. She's only successful on the back of the misery of others. I hate her. She cheated my parents and she cheated me. One day someone will kill her, you mark my words. One day she'll push someone too far."

"And could you be that person, Albert?" I ask. "Could you kill?"

"Moi, Officer? Mais non, I'm as gentle as a lamb," he says feigning hurt, but his eyes tell a different story. His eyes are menacing.

During our conversation, Albert repeats the same story Monsieur Claude told me. It doesn't really give either of them an airtight alibi, because they didn't actually see each other leave and everything they've told me is circumstantial. Their stories don't confirm or deny that Bertrand Dupont was in the building at the same time as either of them, so I'm no further forward in pointing the finger of suspicion. Much as I dislike Albert and find his personality rather threatening, that doesn't make him a murderer.

We part at the river, Albert protesting that I promised him a drink, me ignoring his pleas. As I walk away from him I can still smell the cloying stink of stale alcohol oozing from his pores. It was so overpowering I can taste it. I imagine my clothes and hair smell of him simply from being in his company, and I can't wait to get home and have a shower.

Chapter 12

The rest of the week is spent interviewing the remaining key holders of the spa and some of the other staff as well. By Friday morning, I have spoken to everyone who might have something to tell me and many who know nothing at all. I'm getting desperate. There's only Collette Dupont left to talk to and I don't know what she could possibly add. Still, I'm clutching at straws so I arrange to visit her. I'm dreading Detective Gerard phoning, as I have nothing to report, therefore it's a great relief when I receive an email from him informing me that he'll be away on business for the next ten days. Breathing space, I think, thank goodness. I don't want to be seen to fail.

When I enter the sitting room of Madame Dupont's, I'm aware once again of the many religious icons and ornaments cluttering the shelves and I'm reminded of my mother. She too has a love of all things holy. I'm afraid the symbolism only serves to make me uncomfortable and stirs in me rather negative feelings towards Madame Dupont. My poor relationship with my mother is perhaps making me judge Collette Dupont unfairly, but I can't help it.

"First, let me say that I'm very sorry for your loss," I begin when we're seated. "How are you coping? Do you have someone to help you?"

"My son Emil has come home, so I'm not alone. He'll stay until after the funeral. He's taking it very badly. Emil adored his father," she says. "Bertrand was a good provider, I wanted for nothing and with the insurance policy I'll continue to manage."

"I don't want to upset you," I say. "But could we please discuss what happened in the few days before his death?"

She shifts uncomfortably in her chair and takes a handkerchief from the pocket of her dress. She purses her lips then begins. "I suppose you should know that Bertrand and I had a disagreement and that's why I was at my sister's house in Barcelona. He was very rigid and he liked things to happen in a certain way. His way."

She hugs her arms around her body and rubs her elbows with her hands.

"Can you tell me what this disagreement was about?" I ask.

"Bertrand was troubled about work," she says. He was annoyed that Albert often turned up drunk or incapable, and Bertrand had to cover for his shortcomings. It was very unfair."

A large tear rolls down her cheek and she dabs at it with her handkerchief.

"Then there was the other matter, the number of deaths that have occurred at the spa in the past two months, much more than usual. Bertrand said he was going to bring up the matter with Monsieur Claude. It bothered him that so many people had died from having heart attacks and always in the early morning, before the first treatment sessions had actually begun. It was as if they'd arrived early and immediately dropped dead. They hadn't even had time to change from their outdoor clothes."

More tears roll down her cheeks, more dabbing with the handkerchief. I give her a minute and she blows her nose before continuing.

"I told him not to say anything to Monsieur Claude. It was none of his business and he shouldn't get involved. He was really angry and told me to stay out of it."

She unconsciously touches her cheek.

"Did Bertrand hit you, Madame?" I ask. "Is that why you went to your sister's house?"

Her face reddens then she covers her eyes with her hands. "I'm so ashamed. This wasn't the first occasion Bertrand lost his temper with me, but this time was my own fault, I should have kept out of his affairs."

"I'm sorry to say, Madame, but there is never an excuse for violence. There was nothing you could have said that justified Bertrand's treatment of you."

She nods her head resignedly and dabs again at her eyes. "Thank you," she says. "You are very kind."

"Have you any idea why Bertrand would be wearing his suit?" I ask, changing the subject.

"Perhaps, if he'd arranged a meeting with Monsieur Claude, he might have come home to change from his work clothes first, so he felt on more of an equal footing with him. As I said before, Bertrand was very rigid in his manner and about what he felt was right and proper. It would be just the sort of thing he would do."

I glance at my watch. I'm not going to get any more here, I think. I decide to return to the office and ask Paul to lock up at end of the day, so I can get away early. Gilbert and Stuart will be arriving at our house late in the afternoon, and although Patricia will be organised and ready for their visit, I can't let her cook dinner for six and expect her to greet our guests on her own.

When I'm leaving for home, I detour past the florist on the way to my car so I can buy Patricia some blooms to show her how much I appreciate her. Walking along the street towards the café, I'm alarmed to see Albert sitting at a table drinking with the detective. I wonder what they're up to, I think, immediately remembering my conversation with Collette Dupont about her husband's concerns. As I make my way past them, Albert gives me a thumbs-up sign, and he has an unmistakeable look of triumph on his face.

Chapter 13

I don't think I had any preconceived ideas about how Gilbert and Stuart might look, but I didn't expect them to be so beautiful. Everything, from their designer clothes to their matching luggage, screams Paris. They are elegant, both are tall and slim, but with discernable muscles. Their features are even and they have high cheekbones and strong chins. But for Stuart's fiery red hair, they could be mistaken for brothers. From being a person of some importance in this region, suddenly I feel very provincial, a bit rough round the edges compared to these men, and although Patricia and I are reasonably well-off financially, Gilbert and Stuart are obviously very rich.

Having made the usual introductions and shown them their room, we are now in the lounge area waiting for Patricia to bring coffee. I'm not sure what to say to them, because I don't know anything about them – other than they are a couple and Gilbert is Marjorie's brother. I feel awkward, as if I'm in the company of royalty, when suddenly, the ice is broken by Ollee. For no particular reason, he begins a manic run around and around the room, leaping onto the furniture and our knees as he goes. Both men roar with laughter and when Ollee comes close to Stuart he is grabbed squarely around the middle, Stuart then expertly flips him onto his back and vigorously rubs his belly.

"Do you like that Ollee?" he says. "Do you like that, you wee tyrant?" Ollee yips with delight. "My family have always had dogs," he explains. "There's always at least one attention seeker like this wee mongrel."

He doesn't use the term 'wee mongrel' unkindly, more the reverse. Ollee is not a particularly small dog.

"Do you miss Glasgow, Stuart?" I ask, pleased to finally have something to converse about.

"I certainly don't miss the weather, it rains most days, but I do miss the welcome I get there. In Paris, people can be very cold. We're looking forward to returning to Glasgow, aren't we?" he says and he squeezes Gilbert's knee affectionately. Gilbert blows him a kiss.

It is in that moment when I notice just how camp the men's behaviour is and whilst I have no problem with public displays of affection, our esteemed Mayor will be horrified.

"If you'll excuse me for a minute, please," I say. "I'll just go and help Patricia carry the coffees."

"On you go, we're fine, we're happy playing with Ollee," Gilbert says.

I leave them and go into the kitchen.

"They're really camp. Stuart positively minces when he walks and they keep touching each other on the arm or leg when they talk. They blow each other kisses, for goodness sake," I say to Patricia in a loud whisper.

"They're queer. What did you expect?" she replies.

"I don't know," I admit. "But not this. Francis will have a fit. They can't behave like that at the dance. Everyone will be outraged and Marjorie will be ridiculed. You'll have to talk to them."

"Me? Why me? It's you who's upset. You talk to them."

"I can't talk to them, I barely know them," I protest.

"I don't know them either," she replies.

"Perhaps Marjorie will say something to them later. She'll notice their behaviour at dinner. Let me help you carry the tray," I say. "I don't want them to think we've been talking about them."

* * *

Before very long, Marjorie and Francis arrive and we are all seated at the table. Patricia has excelled herself. Dinner begins with an aperitif, followed by plates of *charcuterie*, *crudites* and a tart made from goat's cheese being placed on the table for everyone to help themselves. The main course is a rich stew of beef cooked in wine. Conversation is flowing and everyone seems relaxed, except of course for Francis. He's used to Patricia, but she makes no display of her sexuality in public, so when he's in her company he can forget that she's a lesbian. Now, however, he's been thrust into a situation where the homosexuals equal the heterosexuals and worse still, Gilbert and Stuart's behaviour is overtly gay.

Francis grows increasingly agitated. He is no longer contributing to the conversation. He's fidgeting with his wedding ring, turning it around and around on his finger.

"Oh, for God's sake! Would you two please stop touching each other? You're putting me off my food," he blurts.

Everyone goes silent, and nobody breathes.

"You can't behave like that in public," Francis continues. "We'll be a laughing stock in this town. You don't see Patricia and Danielle carrying on like that."

More silence.

"Danielle isn't gay," Marjorie finally says.

"And she doesn't fancy me," Patricia adds.

Suddenly, everyone is laughing.

"Oh, you poor wee thing," Stuart says. "Unloved and unwanted."

"I didn't say she doesn't love me. I said she doesn't fancy me."

"That's because she's not gay," Gilbert, Stuart and Marjorie say in unison.

Francis shakes his head in despair.

"I'm sorry," Gilbert says. "We're so used to living in cities like London, Paris and Glasgow. I'd forgotten the reason I left here in the first place. I'd forgotten how damning small town prejudice can be. We'll have to act like real men, so the real men of this town don't feel threatened."

"Maybe you could teach us, Francis," Stuart says."

Francis's face is scarlet. He looks as if his head might explode. He turns to Marjorie and holds up his hands in surrender.

"They're joking, darling," she says. "They're just teasing you. Of course you'll behave appropriately, won't you?" she says, turning to Gilbert. Then she says to me, "Don't let them sit beside each other and for God's sake, do not let them dance together or my husband will have a stroke."

"I don't mind gay people dancing together," Francis says, turning to Gilbert and Stuart. The room grows silent again and we all stare at him in surprise. "Just as long as one of your partners is always Patricia," he adds, attempting to make a joke, but we all know how he really feels and nothing will ever change his opinion.

The dinner progresses and we have eaten our cheese and are enjoying one of Patricia's pies for dessert when Marjorie questions Gilbert. "Is that what you wanted to tell me? Are you and Stuart moving back to live in Glasgow?"

"Yes, that's part of it," Gilbert replies.

"We're getting married," Stuart blurts out, before Gilbert can continue.

"We're declaring our love for each other and our commitment in a civil partnership," Gilbert explains. The men gaze lovingly into each other's eyes and grasp each other's hands. The room is silent.

"Is that legal?" Marjorie asks, finding her voice.

"It's ridiculous, preposterous!" Francis splutters. "How can two men marry?"

"Congratulations," Patricia and I say weakly, almost simultaneously.

"We'd like you all to attend our wedding," Gilbert says.

"Yes," Stuart agrees, nodding enthusiastically. "We want you all to come to Glasgow."

The room is silent once again.

Chapter 14

When we enter the community hall for the dinner dance, I see it has been laid out with long trestle tables and chairs which are covered with coloured cloths to look like the Catalan flag. Each table can hold twenty people and many of the seats have been tilted forward to reserve them for various groups. I see Jean waving furiously at me and signalling for me to come and join him and his party.

"I think Jean has seats for us," I say.

"I'm not sitting with a crowd of municipal workers," Francis grumbles. "I'm already involved with them every working day. Come on Marjorie, we'll go and sit with Remy and Bertha Belmont. They're at a table with Michelle Moliner, the estate agent and that new *notaire*, Pascal Boutiere. The young people can all sit together with the *pompiers*."

"

I can see Marjorie is furious, but not wishing to make a scene, she holds her hands up and shrugs, apologises to Gilbert then runs off after Francis.

"Well, thank goodness for that," Stuart says. "I'm sorry, Gilbert, but your brother-in-law is a boorish bigot. It will be much easier if we don't have to sit with him."

Gilbert looks disappointed and I feel sorry for him, but his mood soon picks up when we join our friends. We stand chatting for a while and drinking sangria, then sit down on either side of the table, one boy beside one girl.

"I thought you two were a couple. Don't you want to sit together? You don't have to worry about this crowd," Jean says with a sweep of his hand. "We're a mixed bunch with no prejudices. I mean just look at us; one black guy from Reunion who's sitting beside his Chinese girlfriend, one Italian who thinks he's a gangster – look at the idiot, wearing his sunglasses indoors. Hey, Marco!" Jean shouts, "We all know you're not the Godfather; take off those ridiculous glasses."

"Yeah, yeah," Marco replies, "And we all know your girlfriend plays rugby better than you do and she calls you sweetie, so don't pretend you're a tough guy."

"Patricia's a lesbian, Danielle's a cop," Jean continues.

"And the Mayor is a bigoted prick," Marco interrupts. "So, leave the poor boy alone. He's trying to impress his family, don't give him a hard time."

"I didn't think we were obviously gay," Gilbert says. "What have we done to give that impression?"

"Well, let me see," Jean begins. "Your boyfriend stands with one hand on his hip while he talks with the other hand, and from time to time, when you're chatting, you flick your hair in a very alluring fashion. Which would be okay if you were a woman, but it's a bit camp for a man," Jean adds.

"Do you think everyone knows?" Gilbert asks, shrinking into his seat. "I couldn't bear it if everyone knew and they shunned us. Marjorie would be devastated."

"Don't worry," Jean reassures him. "You're sitting at a tough table. You're with the *pompiers.*"

At the mention of the word '*pompier*', the whole group stands, raises their glasses and gives a loud cheer. Everyone in the room turns to stare at them. I glance over to the table where the Mayor is seated; his face is like thunder.

"*Pompiers!*" I shout, rousing the crowd again. This time we all stand and cheer, Gilbert and Stuart included.

"You are now honorary members," Jean says and everyone relaxes and is happy.

"Thank you," I whisper to him.

"You owe me," he replies.

The evening progresses and everyone is enjoying themselves. The food is good and there is a seemingly endless supply of wine. Every so often, another jug is brought to the table. I notice that Michelle Moliner is seated at one side of Francis; she is openly flirting with him and Marjorie is not amused, but she is too much of a lady to make a scene. So when the music begins, I go over and ask Francis to dance, giving Marjorie the opportunity to have a quiet but firm word with her.

"I really appreciate what you're doing for me," Francis slurs, he reeks of wine and his tie is stained with what looks like tomato sauce. "Looking after the gay boys, I mean," he adds. "I'll not forget this, Danielle."

Neither will I, I think, as the music ends and I steer him back to his table.

The evening progresses and everybody is enjoying themselves. Our town holds several of these gatherings throughout the year in support of various groups. In the summer, there are several celebrations including a '*sardinade*' where we eat – amongst other things – sardines. In the autumn, fund raisers for everything from the dog's home to the vintage car club – these are usually held outside in the town square. Spring and winter events, such as this one, are held in one of the community halls. The single thing these gatherings all have in common, is our local, all-round entertainer, Emanuel Delfont. He is a legend in these parts and everybody knows that no matter what the age group, if he is entertaining, we can look forward to a fantastic evening.

Nearly everyone is on the dance floor and Marjorie is dancing with Pascal, the *notaire*, when a very drunken Albert reels over to her and grabs her by the arm. They are standing quite close to our table.

"Why are you with him, when you could be with me?" Albert shouts, his voice rising above the music. "I'm stronger than him and I'm much better looking."

"Drunker than him," someone quips.

"Uh oh, trouble brewing," I say as the music stops. "Come on guys. I think I'll need your help."

Surprisingly, Gilbert is the first on his feet.

"Please don't get hurt," Stuart pleads. "Gilbert's got a quick temper," he explains.

"That's my sister the oaf has his hands on," Gilbert says, his face flushed with anger.

When Albert sees a group of us coming towards him, he immediately releases Marjorie's arm.

"Sorry, I'm sorry, I love this lady. She's kind and decent," he slurs. "Not like my bitch of a cousin. Not like Michelle-fucking-Moliner. And not like him," he says, pushing the *notaire* on the shoulder, almost knocking him to the ground. "Or him," he adds, pointing to Monsieur Claude who has edged forward to see what's going on. "They're all bandits, thieves. They're all out to rob us. The detective knows. He knows what you're up to, you bunch of bandits. He knows and so do I."

With a flailing attempt to swing a punch at the *notaire*, Albert misses and falls to the floor unconscious.

Jean and a couple of his friends lift the comatose man by his clothes and carry him unceremoniously towards the door, with his toes dragging on the parquet.

"Shows over, folks," I say. "He's had his last dance," I add and people chuckle.

The music restarts but the mood has changed. The evening is beginning to wind down.

"Have you any idea what that was all about?" Patricia asks when we are seated back at the table.

"He was just drunk," I reply.

But I couldn't help noticing the glances which passed between Moliner, Claude and Boutiere while Albert was kicking off. And what, I wonder, do Albert and the detective know that I do not? Something is going on and I intend to find out what it is. First thing on Monday morning, I plan to have a little chat with Gregory Armand before he disappears back to Beziers.

Chapter 15

The phone rings at 10am on Sunday morning, but it didn't wake us as we are all already up. Stuart is still eating breakfast, although the rest of us have finished and are just drinking coffee. Stuart has a huge appetite and a very sweet tooth. He's still stuffing himself with baguette. He has, in fact, eaten a whole baguette on his own and is now sampling a third type of Patricia's preserves.

"I don't know where he puts it," Gilbert says. "Look at him. There's not a gram of spare flesh anywhere, and I should know," he adds with a wink.

"Cheeky! You're just jealous," Stuart replies and he keeps munching.

"It's Marjorie on the phone," I say to Gilbert, interrupting the banter. "She wants to speak to you."

Gilbert rolls his eyes. "Probably some more criticism from your esteemed Mayor," he says as he reaches for the receiver.

"Will you manage to come to Glasgow for our wedding?" Stuart asks. "It's an amazing city with lots of things to do and see."

"I've heard there are many examples of artwork by Charles Rennie Mackintosh," Patricia says. "I love his work. He lived in this region for a while, you know."

"Yes, I was aware of that," Stuart replies. "But the difference is that here you pay a fortune to visit a tiny gallery, whereas in

Glasgow, all the museums and galleries are free. You'd love it, Patricia, you'd be in your element."

"We will try to attend," I say and Patricia's eyes sparkle. "Once you've firmed up the arrangements, let us know. We've travelled to London before, so Glasgow won't be a problem."

"Thanks," Stuart says. "Gilbert doesn't expect his family to come, apart from Marjorie, of course. He's very disappointed that I haven't yet met her children. My family are so accepting of us. I guess that's the difference between a modern city and small town France."

What he says is true and is not meant to be unkind, but it stings. It makes me feel as if I live in a backwater where the people are ignorant hicks. It belittles me and my way of life.

"Marjorie would like to treat us all to lunch in Camprodon. Would you like to go?" Gilbert calls over to us. "At about two o'clock, at the restaurant beside the river. She says she'll pick me and Stuart up if you two have other plans."

"I'd love to," Patricia says to me. "If you are willing to drive us and the boys, we could leave early and go to the market. Then we can have a wander around town before we meet up with Marjorie and Francis."

"Tell Marjorie, yes, thanks," I reply. "We'll meet them there."

Before very long we are in my car driving up the mountain towards Spain. The narrow road with its sickening twists and turns and dramatic, sheer drops has Stuart squealing and whimpering.

"Did I tell you I don't like heights?" he cries.

"Don't be such a wimp. There are hardly ever any accidents," Gilbert says. "Well, perhaps one or two," he concedes. "But only during the car rallies. Then people drive like maniacs."

"Just don't look down," Patricia suggests.

It doesn't help. By the time we reach Camprodon, Stuart is the colour of a lime and I know he'll be worse on the way back when every corner makes you feel as if you're about to be launched into space. It's such a shame that he's frightened, because the countryside is spectacular with its tree-covered peaks and valleys, sporting a million shades of green.

We enter town and drive past chalet style apartments; it resembles a Swiss ski resort, but when we're at the centre, with its narrow old streets, the town is most definitely Catalan. The market square is small but bustling, and within minutes Patricia is haggling for fruit and vegetables while the boys have wandered into a shop and are oohing and ahhing over crockery. I take myself further down the street to my favourite shop and spend the next half hour sampling and choosing cheese. Then I wander on to a supermarket to buy a bottle of gin because it's cheaper in Spain and the boys practically cleaned us out on Friday. Before very long, we are all shopped out and the boot of the car is laden.

"If we lived in a town like this I'd be the size of a house," Stuart says, marvelling at the range of specialist food shops.

"No, I'd be the size of a house and you'd still be slim," Gilbert says. "Life's so unfair."

Patricia and I laugh at the comfortable way the boys bicker. They seem so natural together. All of us are dreading lunch with Francis.

"What time is your train this evening?" I ask when we are all together and seated at a table.

"Not until nine-thirty," Gilbert replies. "I do hope we'll have time for Stuart to meet the children," he adds. "It would be a shame for us to come all this way and miss them."

"I think they're dining with friends tonight," Francis says without looking up from his food. "You know how children are," he adds. "They're friends are always much more important to them than family get-togethers."

"Of course Stuart will meet them," Marjorie retorts. "I've told them to be home by six and wait for us. You're their uncle, Gilbert and they want to spend time with you and meet Stuart, even if it's just for a short time."

I glance around the table. Gilbert is beaming. Stuart and Patricia are surprised. Marjorie looks triumphant. Francis looks sick. I guess we now know who the true boss of that family is, I think.

The restaurant is very classy with the waiters smartly clad in black uniforms. The menu is superb. For starters, we choose *croquettas* made from a variety of fillings such as fish, chicken or beef and *cannelonis* stuffed with wild boar – all typically Catalan. This is followed by a choice of main course which includes duck, lamb, oxtail, chicken or cod served in various ways. The dessert table is, in Stuart's words, "to die for" and he has two servings. By the time the coffees are served with petit fours, we are ready for a siesta. The bill is not small, but Francis insists on paying for everyone. He looks at Marjorie rather sheepishly, but she is obviously still not ready to forgive him for trying to manipulate her and their children and she doesn't return his look with a smile. After a stroll along the river to try to walk off some of the food we've eaten, we say our goodbyes to Marjorie and Francis and drive back down the mountain so the boys can pack. Fortunately, Stuart sleeps all the way home.

"Well then, what did you think of Marjorie?" Gilbert asks when I park outside the house. "Wasn't she amazing? She was like that when we were growing up, you know. She always got her way."

"I think, perhaps, Francis and the children will be attending your wedding after all," I reply.

"You might be right," Gilbert replies happily. "You might very well be right."

Chapter 16

First thing on Monday morning, Gregory Armand arrives at the office to speak to me so there is no need to telephone him. It seems he has more unanswered questions than I do and I'm concerned. I don't like strangers digging around in my patch and I hope that after our little chat, he leaves town. When we are seated, I offer him coffee but he declines, another bad sign. It's clear he means business and doesn't want to be distracted by niceties.

"If you don't mind, Officer," he says. "I'll tell you what I know and what I want to find out, then we can go on from there."

I nod. I much prefer asking the questions, but in this instance, I might learn more from just listening.

"There is no dispute that Madame Falandry died, and before she died her home was gifted to Monsieur Claude. The death was witnessed by a Doctor Poullet and by Monsieur Claude, both of whom were present at the spa shortly before opening time. Doctor Poullet pronounced Madame Falandry dead of a heart attack. She had been, at that time, quite recently diagnosed with terminal cancer, but she had no prior evidence of heart disease. Are you with me so far?" he asks.

I nod in agreement but say nothing.

"Monsieur Falandry is not happy with this information. He asked me to enquire about having the body exhumed and a post-mortem carried out, but when I contacted the funeral home they advised me that only her ashes have been interred in her family crypt. Madame Falandry had been cremated. The funeral home also informed me that Monsieur Claude paid for her funeral and he had all the relevant paperwork giving him permission to deal with her body in any way he saw fit. Knowing there was a family crypt, why would he choose to have her body cremated?"

"Perhaps it was easier and cheaper to move her ashes than to move her corpse," I suggest. "He assumed she had no living family."

"Perhaps," he agrees. "Now, let us throw in another complication. On receipt of the 'gift' Monsieur Claude almost immediately sells the house for slightly lower than market value, probably in order to get a quick sale. But the transaction is not, as one would expect, dealt with by an estate agent and *notaire* working in the vicinity where the house is situated. Instead the sale is handled by Michelle Moliner, using your local *notaire*, Pascal Boutiere."

He pauses to let this information sink in before continuing. "Within a few days of receiving the money, Monsieur Claude buys a substantial property from Michelle Moliner. A property previously owned by the parents of Albert, the assistant caretaker of the spa. Albert believes that he's been cheated out of his inheritance by Michelle Moliner, with the assistance of the *notaire*."

He pauses again. I stand and pour myself a coffee, offering one to Monsieur Armand once again.

"I think I will have one now, thank you," he says and I set a cup on the table in front of him. "Then," he continues. "There is the untimely death of Bertrand Dupont."

"What could he possibly have to do with the death of Madame Falandry?" I ask. "I checked and he wasn't even working on the day she died."

"Perhaps nothing," Armand replies. "But I spoke to his wife and she told me that he was troubled by the amount of sudden deaths occurring in a short period of time. One of those deaths was Madame Falandry." He sips his coffee. "I'm particularly worried about the involvement of the doctor. He witnessed Madame Falandry's death, then he signed the death certificate and the papers releasing the body for cremation. Why was he even at the spa so early in the morning?"

I cannot offer him any explanation. We sit staring at each other for a moment, then he says, "I'm planning to drive back to Beziers this afternoon so I can report my findings to Monsieur Falandry, but I'll return here in a couple of days. When I do, I'll probably be asking you to investigate Doctor Poullet. At the very least, I need to know why he was the only official person involved. Surely after witnessing the death, he should have called for another doctor?"

"This is a small town, Monsieur," I say. "Doctor Poullet is the man one calls. I can assure you, he is very well respected."

"Maybe that's true, but this whole business feels wrong and I intend to tie up all the loose ends."

After Armand leaves, I sit with my head in my hands and contemplate what he's told me. There is no concrete evidence to suggest any wrongdoing, but there are inconsistencies. My old friend, Poullet, is a pain in the ass, but he's always looked after his patients superbly and everyone sings his praises. I do hope this troublemaker from Bezier doesn't try to cause him any grief.

Chapter 17

After everyone returns from lunch, I decide to go to Poullet's surgery to have a chat with him, but Marcel informs me that he's just passed him in the street, walking towards the covered car park beside the spa. I know he should be working today, so I assume he's probably just collecting something from his car.

"Mind the office, Paul," I say. "I'll take a walk around to the car park and try to head Poullet off."

"Okay, Boss," he replies. "But just remember, being on the pavement won't protect you if he's driving. That man's car has had more bumps than a dodgem."

Although Paul is making a joke, he's not far wrong. I once saw Poullet trying to do a three-point turn. It took six attempts and involved hitting the kerb several times, along with a garden gate and a litter bin.

"I'll try to avoid being killed, but if I don't return, I bequeath you Laurent," I reply. "You deserve some aggravation for being such a smartass."

Laurent is attempting to throw a screwed-up ball of paper into the wastepaper bin but keeps missing. Over and over he rises from his chair to retrieve it and try again.

"Oh, for God's sake," I say with annoyance and, as I walk past his desk, lift the ball of paper and lob it into the bin. "Have you got nothing better to do?"

Laurent lowers his gaze and shuffles some files on his desk. Paul stifles a laugh and continues typing something into his computer. Marcel looks as if he's about to say something, but I silence him with a glare and he too, shuffles papers trying to look busy.

I sigh as I leave the confines of the office, breathing deeply in the cool, fresh air as I make my way through town towards the car park. The sun is shining so brightly it makes me blink, and I have to fish around in my shoulder bag for sunglasses. A delicious smell of newly-baked bread reaches my nostrils and I can't avoid detouring past the *boulangerie* to buy some croissants. As I come out of the shop, my friend Byron calls to me from across the street.

"Bonjour, Danielle, time for a coffee?" he asks. "I wanted to ask you a small favour," he adds.

I'm torn between duty and desire, but in the end duty wins and I reply, "No to the coffee. Yes, to the favour. I'll catch up with you later."

"But you don't yet know what I'm going to ask of you," he protests.

"It doesn't matter," I call back. "For you, dear, anything."

Byron is one of my best friends and I would move heaven and earth to help him, but I am intrigued. I'll have to get in touch with him later to find out what he wants.

When I arrive at the car park it's in chaos. The person at the front of the queue, who is trying to exit, is having difficulty with her swipe card. People who pay for annual parking simply use their card for entering and exiting, but sometimes the magnetic strip is compromised, as it appears to be on this occasion, and all hell breaks loose. Drivers are getting out of their vehicles and shouting at the poor woman who is stuck.

"We can't hang around all day! Some of us have to get to work," one red-faced man shouts.

"I also have work to attend!" she replies, sounding exasperated. "Do you think I like wasting my time with this stupid machine?"

"Where do you keep your card?" another woman enquires. "Because if you keep it in your purse with your keys, it damages the magnetic strip."

A couple of people agree with her and strike up a conversation about the sensitivity of magnetic strips and how useless computers are, but it does nothing to ease the current situation.

"Where is the attendant?" the one who's stuck asks anyone who'll listen. "Someone is meant to be here to help us if there's a problem."

I'm lying low, hiding behind a pillar because I don't want to get roped in. There's nothing I can do to assist them, as only the attendant can lift the gate barring their way. I carefully skirt around the problem and make my way inside using the pedestrian entrance. When I enter the covered parking area, it feels damp and smells dank. The light is very low and it takes my eyes a moment to adjust before I'm disappointed to see that Doctor Poullet's private parking bay is empty. When I turn to leave, I practically bump into Monsieur Claude in the gloom. He's wiping his hands on a rag and I can detect a pungent odour coming from it.

"Having a problem with your car?" I enquire.

"Um, not really," he replies, "Just the usual, checking the oil and water and filling the windscreen washer."

"I've been speaking to Gregory Armand," I say. "He's got a lot of questions about Madame Falandry. He also mentioned something about an apartment block you've recently purchased, something to do with Albert's parents. Is there anything I should know?"

"Pah, that man is an idiot. I've done nothing wrong. I bought that building from the estate agency. All the paperwork is in order. I plan to renovate it and then let it out to 'curists' visiting the spa. I'm going to need some assistance with planning permission for the changes I want to make. Actually, I was hoping to see you. I'd like to discuss a business proposition with you when you have the time."

He's still rubbing his hands on the wet smelly rag and he seems a bit agitated.

"You want me for a business proposition?" I repeat. "I hope it doesn't involve money," I joke.

Although Patricia and I are comfortably off, I don't want anyone to know our circumstances.

He shakes his head. "No, Danielle, don't worry, I don't need your money, just your input. On the contrary, this opportunity will make you money. How about we meet up after the holidays to discuss it? No obligation, just a talk."

"Yes, okay, we'll do that," I reply. "So long as you know that my investigation into Dupont's death is a separate issue. I cannot allow one thing to influence another."

"Absolutely," he replies. "Hopefully, this whole business will be behind us soon. Hopefully that idiot detective will go away and not come back."

I wish for that too, but I have a feeling in my guts that we haven't heard the last of Gregory Armand.

Chapter 18

Jesus the kitten has been re-homed with Sarah, the expert on all things fluffy and furry. Mimi's interest in him disappeared almost as soon as it started. In fact, she became irritated with him and may have hurt him, had Patricia not intervened. I am relieved; there are enough animals to care for and I have more than enough responsibilities already. Patricia was upset for a day or two, but has stopped talking about it now.

I'm helping Byron by driving to a *brocante* in Ceret. He's located an antique chest that he wishes to purchase. Byron says it's a genuine Louis the Fifteenth, marble-topped commode and worth a small fortune. It will fit into the back of my car with the seats down. Byron doesn't want to entrust it to a removal man with a van, and when he tells me its price, I don't blame him. Why anyone would pay so much money for an old piece of brown furniture is beyond my comprehension, but what do I know about antiques?

Many *brocantes* in France stock a wide range of items that purport to be antiques, and while some are the genuine article, others things are simply old. Nothing is thrown away, even if it's damaged. Everything has a price and a fool who wants to pay it. Some people believe that the more woodworm a piece of furniture has, the more antique it must be, and therefore the higher its value.

This particular shop is packed with items; so many things, it's hard to move. The angry face of a stuffed, wild boar stares down from its mount on one wall – incongruously, a small ornate, glass lampshade is perched on its head. No wonder it's annoyed. Further along the same wall is a stag's head, its antlers hung with Christmas tree baubles. Attached to the wall between these poor creatures are paintings and photographs, hats and helmets, swords and fishing rods – there is no order to anything. On the floor are pieces of furniture and rails full of vintage clothes. Tables covered with an assortment of glass and china items labelled '*Sevres*', '*Daum*' and '*Lalique*' fill every inch of space; under these tables, are copper pots, woodworking tools, baskets of linen and boxes of handbags and scarves. I have no idea how Byron managed to identify a valuable piece of furniture in such a place. To me, it looks like a shop full of old junk.

"Bonjour, Monsieur, Madame; how nice to see you again Monsieur," a very petite and pretty blonde lady says. She has stepped out from behind a carved rosewood cabinet. I jump with surprise because I didn't realise she was there.

"I startled you. I'm so sorry, Madame. I didn't realise Monsieur had a wife. Such a dignified man, your husband, you are very lucky. My husband had been gone for five years. I miss not having a man in my life," she says.

I am about to put her right when Byron places his arm around my shoulder and gives me a squeeze.

"Ah, yes Madame, a good partner is a wonderful asset," he replies.

"Don't say a word," he hisses in my ear. "Or I might end up with more than I bargained for. I think she fancies me. Maybe that's why the price of the commode was so good."

We inspect the piece of furniture in question. They talk at length about the quality of the marquetry and the handles and the serpentine shape and the rose-coloured, marble top until I'm bored numb. I sigh and wind my way around the shop a couple of times, but still they are talking. Finally, Byron has his cheque book out and is paying the woman. She keeps chatting and smiling and touching his arm, and I fear we'll be here all day if I don't intervene.

"I'm sorry, darling," I say to Byron. "But remember I have an appointment in Perpignan. We need to leave now or I'll be late," I lie, and I glare at him to let him know I've had enough.

He flinches, checks his watch. "Is that the time? Sorry, dear girl, of course we must get going."

With much puffing and panting and moving of this and that, finally the commode is out of the shop, wrapped in a dust sheet, carefully stowed in my car and we are on our way.

"I'm sorry if I made you late, Danielle. I get a bit carried away in antique shops. To most people, they're dark and dingy places that smell of damp and dust, but to me, they have the sweet aroma of money and opportunity."

I feel a bit guilty for rushing Byron. He's a good friend and I know he'd help me if I needed his assistance.

"It's not a problem, Byron. I just need to get into the office to instruct my staff, or they'll do nothing all morning. They're a lazy bunch, I'm afraid."

"And how are things going with your investigation? Are you any further on? I've heard a detective from Beziers is poking around."

"We're still not a hundred percent sure Dupont's death wasn't simply a tragic accident. As for the detective, he's on a fishing trip about a completely different matter. He's left town now anyway. That's one less thing for me to deal with," I reply.

The journey takes a bit longer than usual because I'm very aware of my valuable cargo, but soon we are at Byron's house and between us, we manhandle the commode into his sitting room. I'm about to leave when Byron hands me a small package.

"What's this?" I ask.

"For you, dear girl, my small way of saying thank you."

"You didn't have to give me anything," I protest. "We're friends."

He smiles shyly, "And I appreciate our friendship very much. Open it, see if you like it. I think it's to your taste."

I tear open the wrapping paper and lift the lid off the small box to reveal an elegant silver bracelet with a little heart-shaped charm attached. It's exactly my taste and style.

"Oh, Byron, I love it, but it's far too much. You shouldn't have." I lean forward and kiss him on both cheeks. "Thank you. Thank you so much."

"Oh, if I were only twenty years younger and a bit better looking," he replies, smiling. He has a twinkle in his eye. "You really are a darling girl."

"Right, I'd better get moving," I say, changing the subject and breaking the slight awkwardness. "By the way, what are you doing for Christmas? Are you going back to England?"

"I'm not sure what I'm doing," he replies and I detect sadness in his voice. "My daughter and her family are spending the holidays with their friends in Amsterdam, so I'll just have to see how things turn out."

We say our goodbyes. By the time I reach the office, I've decided to phone Patricia and ask if I may invite Byron to dine with us at Christmas. It's not a time for being alone and besides, he's such good company. Patricia's already suggested we invite my parents. I know my father will want to dine with us, but I'm not sure about my mother as we rarely see each other and we don't get on. However, if they do decide to come, Byron's presence might just save the day.

Chapter 19

The dry, icy wind cuts through my wool jacket and chills my bones. I'm glad I chose to wear my scarf, gloves and the ridiculous, over-sized, Russian-style hat with ear flaps that Patricia bought me for mornings such as this. She thinks it makes me look cute, but right now, I don't care how I look as long as I'm warm. When I switch on the car engine the temperature gauge reads four degrees. The season has definitely changed and winter is upon us. The windscreen, which I first thought was covered in frost, is just grubby and streaky. I clean it before I set off. At least I can drive with my headlights on for part of the way, as I'm unlikely to meet many other cars this early in the morning. The sky is very dark, and as much of my journey is without the benefit of street lamps, I feel safer with a full beam to light my way.

I'm driving to the vineyard of our friends, Anna and Frederick. Patricia and I assisted them with their grape harvest in September and we are being paid for our labour with wine. Twenty-four bottles await me and I'm going to fetch them to consume over the holidays. Racing along the road I break the speed limit, crossing the central line at the bends, every few miles a sensor lights up a speed sign advising me how fast I'm travelling, but I don't care. My visibility is good and besides, there is nobody on duty at this ungodly hour to book me.

By the time dawn has broken and the sun is rising, the vineyard is stretching out before me. Gnarled, ancient stumps grow in straight lines for as far as my eyes can see. I'd forgotten how many vines grew on this flat plain and how backbreaking the harvest was. The wine had better be good – I've earned it, I think to myself.

Normally, I prefer being in the mountains. I like the feeling of being surrounded by them, of being contained and safe, but recently I've felt hemmed in. Working towards the end of the year with an unsolved case on my books is frustrating, unsettling, but I cannot see any way to finally bury Bertrand Dupont. I am sure he was murdered. It's obvious he was murdered, but I can't prove what happened and I have no suspect to pursue. According to the statements I've received, he was alone in an empty building, which was locked. It's like the old riddle, 'Who killed Henri?' He was killed in an empty, locked room, but of course it turns out Henri was a goldfish not a man, and he was eaten by the cat.

Then there is Gregory Armand and his investigations. There is probably no mystery regarding Madame Falandry – just a greedy husband and a detective trying to earn his fee – but what about her house? I have never heard of such a thing. The house always passes to the next of kin. Why would she gift it to Claude, just prior to her death? Her death was expected, but not imminent. Did she have a premonition that she would be struck down with a heart attack before the cancer killed her?

It's been a struggle for me to reach the position I now enjoy, both in my work and my private life. I want to end the year on a high note with nothing outstanding, but as the days' tick away, it seems less and less likely.

When I arrive at Anna and Freddy's, I park my car in the yard beside the house, climb out and breathe in the cold air. The wind has died down but I can taste frost when I inhale. As I reach the farmhouse the door is thrown open and I'm drawn in to the main room by Anna who hugs me and kisses me. Frederick rises from his seat and he too embraces me, making a great show of planting smacking kisses on my cheeks.

"Danielle, our dear friend, our saviour in time of need," Freddy says dramatically. "Welcome, welcome, sit down here at the stove and get warm. Your cheeks are freezing."

The house is serene and comfortable, like an archetypal scene from a Christmas card. A long, solid wooden table surrounded by a hotchpotch of mismatched chairs fills the central space. Gleaming pots and pans hang from hooks above the stone sink and a dresser laden with china stands solidly against the wall beside it. A large stove takes prime position against the side wall. It warms the whole room. Their little dog is sitting on a handmade, rag rug in front of the stove, gnawing on a bone. He greets me with a small wag of his tail, but doesn't break from his task. Four over-stuffed armchairs, piled with homemade cushions, fill the space in front of the stove. A basket of logs rests beside the stove, and before he takes his seat, Freddy selects one, opens the stove door, rakes the ashes and pushes the log into the fire. A flurry of little sparks fly up and twinkle like stars as he manoeuvres the log into place. The wood smoke smells sweet.

"That's your wine over there," Freddy says, pointing to the four cardboard boxes standing in the corner of the room. "I think you'll enjoy it. We've been rewarded well for all our work."

"Yes, we can relax now," Anna says. "All the work's done until the spring. The basket that's on top of the boxes is a little Christmas gift for you and Patricia, nothing much I'm afraid, just some produce for your table."

"I have your gift in the car," I say. "I forgot to bring it in. Some of Patricia's preserves and pies for the holidays."

I kept their gift in the car because I didn't want to embarrass them if they hadn't got one for us.

"I'll just go and fetch it," I say rising from my chair.

When I re-enter the room, I place their gift on the table and sit down. Anna has placed baguettes, croissants, butter, cheese and jam on the table. She is pouring coffee into large, robust mugs. The scene is one of delightful, domestic harmony and I'll be sorry when I must leave and go to work. The little dog stands, stretches until his tail shakes, then sniffs the air. There are better tasty morsels available now, so he's abandoned his bone and instead positions himself at my side and rests his head on my knee.

"Just ignore him, Danielle, or he'll charm the food right out of your mouth," Freddy says. "He's a rogue. Don't be fooled by those eyes."

What he says is true I know – I too have a dog who is charming, but still I sneak small pieces of croissant to the little animal.

For the next hour, I stuff myself with their good food and coffee, share in conversation and soak up the warmth of their home, but all good things must come to an end and if I don't leave now, I might stay forever. Freddy helps me carry the wine to my car and it is with a heavy heart that I put the key in the ignition and start the engine. As I drive away, I look in my rear-view mirror. I see lights twinkling in the windows of the farmhouse and Freddy and Anna waving to me from the doorway. I envy the simplicity of the day that stretches before them and dread the day that faces me.

Chapter 20

The closer it gets to Christmas, the happier people become. They enjoy banter and bartering, shopping for gifts and gastronomy, smiling and even singing as they go about their business. Everyone is cheerful, it seems – everyone except me. I mope, I moan, and I wearily drag myself around because I can't get the answers I need and it's driving me mad. I think that nothing can get any worse, then suddenly and unexpectedly, it does. We receive a call from Monsieur Falandry. Marcel puts him through.

"Bonjour, bonjour, am I speaking to the senior officer?"

"Bonjour, Monsieur," I say. "Can I help you?" My heart is pounding in my chest. Does Falandry know something? Has Gregory Armand given him the answers that elude me?

"Pardon, Madame," he says politely, "but I asked to speak to the most senior officer. Can you put me through to him, please?"

"I am the most senior officer, Monsieur," I reply wearily. "If you wish to speak to a male officer, if there is something of a sensitive nature you want to discuss, I'll let you speak to my assistant."

I know he's just being a typical chauvinist. I come across his type all the time. They always assume the senior officer will be a man.

"Sorry, forgive me please, I just thought…" his voice trails off.

I sit in silence, waiting for him to resume speaking.

"I'm calling about a Monsieur Gregory Armand," he begins. "He telephoned me to inform me that he was driving to Prats for an appointment at the hotel, before returning here to Beziers. He has failed to turn up. I've called his landlady, she hasn't seen him since he left to travel to your town several days ago. I telephoned the hotel and was informed he left there immediately after his appointment. He told the receptionist he was heading home to Beziers. I want to report him as a missing person."

"Monsieur," I reply. "He's been gone for only a couple of days. Perhaps he went to meet someone, somewhere else. You might not be his only client. Maybe we should wait a few days more before panicking."

"No, Officer, you don't understand. He told me he had information for me and he wanted to give it to me and pick up his cheque before I leave for Tenerife. I'm going on holiday with my girlfriend," he explains. "Tomorrow morning," he adds pointedly. "Gregory needs the money. He said he was short of cash so he would definitely come straight back here to collect it. I'm sure something is wrong. I'm worried something has happened to him."

There's a chill in the pit of my stomach. "Monsieur," I say. "Don't worry about Monsieur Armand, I'll locate him. You go and enjoy your holiday. People change their plans all the time. They don't realise how disturbing a lack of communication can be. From my experience, I can tell you, they usually turn up and are surprised to find that everyone is searching for them."

I can tell by his reaction that Falandry is not totally convinced, but he leaves me his mobile number and accepts what I've said.

When I hang up the phone, my stomach is churning and I feel rather sick. From what Falandry has told me, I too think Gregory Armand might be in trouble. As I come out of my room into the main office, I hear the guys chatting. When they notice me, the conversation abruptly ends and they look at me expectantly.

"Well, Boss," Paul asks, "Anything new?"

"Gregory Armand took a trip up the mountain but he didn't come down," I reply. "He's disappeared."

"Fuck," says Paul. The others remain silent. "Do you think something's happened to him?"

"I just don't know," I reply. "But at the very least, I'll have to drive to Prats and check out what Fallandry's just told me. He's reported Armand as a missing person. Fancy a drive?" I add.

"Yes, okay," Paul says, standing, "but we'd better take your car, Boss. A four-wheel drive will have much better road holding on those winding mountain tracks than my old wreck."

"It's about an hour's drive each way and you've got about three hours of daylight left," Laurent observes. "You should be able to see any marks on the road or the mountainside."

"You think he might have come off the road?" I question.

"Maybe," Laurent replies. "There are a couple of hairpin bends, where the road is very narrow. If he was in a hurry, driving fast and not used to the area, who knows?"

"Fuck," Paul repeats. "We'd better get going, Boss, before the light fades. Laurent's right – there are a few narrow, bendy bits. No fun to drive on in the dark, especially in winter."

"Are you planning on coming back?" Laurent asks. "Do you want me to lock up tonight?"

Paul throws him his set of keys. "Here are my keys, just in case. If I don't come back, you can have my desk."

Laurent looks shocked. "I didn't mean…" he starts, then lapses into an uncomfortable silence.

Marcel laughs nervously.

"Idiot," I say, flicking Paul's ear. "Come on, let's get moving."

We chat as I drive. Paul tells me his mother has thirteen people for Christmas dinner.

"It'll be like the last supper," he says. "Personally, I can't be bothered with all the carry-on and all that fuss and expense for just one day. Then in January there's *la fete des rois*, then Epiphany and another round of gifts and meals. It's too much."

"It's easier for Patricia and me, because we have no children involved. On Christmas Day we plan to have my mother and father and perhaps one very close friend over. Mind you, my mother can be extremely difficult. Though I do enjoy *la fete des rois* in January and eating the *galettes des rois*," I add. "And my friend is a marvellous cook and baker."

"Don't get me wrong," Paul continues. "I liked it when I was a child and it was all about me. But now I'm expected to play with my sister's kids and entertain my young cousin and, quite frankly, I'd much rather get drunk and fall asleep in a chair like my father."

"That sounds like my sort of Christmas," I reply.

Paul raises his eyebrows. "You're a lucky devil," he replies. "I hope you appreciate that."

We continue driving, carefully studying the road for any tell-tale signs of an accident and we have almost reached Prats when Paul asks me to pull in.

"Look, Boss – there on the road, black skid marks, tyre tracks."

"I'll need to get to a passing point. It's too narrow to stop here," I reply.

Rounding the next bend, I see a suitable place about fifty yards ahead. We've been lucky, I think. I let Paul out of the car and park as close to the mountainside as I can, then I put on the hazard lights and pop the boot. Paul lifts out the triangle and places it appropriately as a warning to other drivers. I don't want some-one coming around the corner and ploughing into my car. We start to walk back down the hill.

"Oh, mon Dieu, would you look at that," Paul says, pointing to marks on the side of the mountain. "Someone has come down here at high speed, on the wrong side of the road and scraped their car the whole length along the rock."

"I think whoever did this must have been terrified," I say. "I think they've been trying to slow down or stop their vehicle by running it along the mountainside. The road has been too narrow and they've been going too fast for them to get a good angle. The careering car has scraped along until it reached that bend," I suggest, pointing ahead. "Then the protrusion of rock, instead of stopping them, might have launched them over the side. You can see the skid marks where the car has been tilted onto two wheels. They've probably pulled on the handbrake as a last resort, but have been going too fast for it to do any good."

We walk to the edge of the road and peer down. I've never been keen on heights, but the trees growing all the way down the mountainside soften the impact of the view.

"Fuck," says Paul.

"Merde," I say. "There, in the trees. Can you see it Paul? Something's broken the branches and is stuck in the trees."

"Fuck," he repeats. "Move along a bit and we'll get a better view."

We edge along, holding onto each other, trying to peer down without falling over the drop. "Oh. Sweet Jesus, it's a car," Paul says. "There's a branch right through the middle of it. That's what's stopped it from falling all the way down to the bottom. If it's Armand, the poor soul is mince. It must have been there for a couple of days. The whole thing is a mangled mess, no one would have seen it unless they were actually searching for it because the pine trees have hidden it from view."

"Call the *pompiers*, Paul. Ask for a mountain rescue team to be sent, we have to get him out. But there's probably no rush," I add sadly. "The car is smashed to pieces, stuck half way up a tree in winter. The poor man never stood a chance."

I had hoped to hear no more from Gregory Armand – but not in this way and particularly, not in my jurisdiction.

The sky clouds over, an icy wind is blowing and it has started to rain when I receive a call to inform me that help is only ten minutes away. The dispatcher explains that road blocks have been set up in both directions to turn back traffic. I was wondering why no cars had passed us; now I know. A person can get cold very quickly on the mountain because it is high up and exposed, so we return to the car to wait. Sure enough, within ten minutes, we hear sirens approaching. Jerome, the man in charge, politely introduces himself to me before he quickly assesses the situation with the aid of binoculars.

"The conditions are deteriorating fast," he says. "We won't be able to retrieve the vehicle today. I'll send two men down the slope on harnesses to check for any casualties and we'll have to call it a day until first light tomorrow."

"I'm expecting you to find one occupant," I reply. "Monsieur Gregory Armand. If I'm correct, he'll have been down there for two days so you're more likely looking at a corpse than a casualty."

It takes nearly twenty minutes for the men to put on all their equipment and set up the pulley system. The sky has darkened and the *pompiers* are using powerful lamps to light the mountainside. Paul and I are now shivering with the cold. Finally, they begin their descent and within a minute they've disappeared from our view into the trees. We wait and we wait as the minutes' tick by. Paul and I are so chilled, we're shamelessly hugging each other to keep warm. Then there's a tug on the rope and a shout and the men are raised back up.

"One body," the first man reports. "We won't be able to retrieve it without cutting equipment because a tree branch has impaled it to the seat of the car. I couldn't photograph the corpse for identification, because it's been decapitated by a second branch. The head will be somewhere on the floor at the rear of the vehicle, I think."

I'm horrified by what I've heard, but the man is very matter-of-fact. I suppose he often has to deal with terrible scenes and has become hardened to them.

"We found this," the second man says, handing me a man's wallet. It is smeared with blood. "I think it's your guy, Officer. There are business cards inside in the name of Gregory Armand."

Paul draws a plastic bag from his pocket and I drop the wallet into it.

"There's nothing else we can do tonight," Jerome says. "My men will tape off the area and place accident warning signs on the road. I'll call you tomorrow, when we get the car up. I've put in a call for a Doctor Lacroix to attend. He'll pronounce the body and take care of it. I'll give him your contact details. We'll have to inspect the car to see if we can find any obvious faults, such as problems with the brakes or steering, so I'll have it taken to the police garage. But for now, we can call it a night."

I thank Jerome, shake his hand and say goodbye, before Paul and I run to my car. When we jump inside, I turn on the engine and put the heater on full blast.

"I don't think I'll ever feel warm again," Paul says, shivering.

"Actually, you will," I reply. "But that poor stiff halfway down the mountain will be stone cold for eternity."

Chapter 21

I phone Falandry first thing in the morning and catch him before he leaves for Tenerife.

"I'm sorry, Monsieur," I say. "We've located a car we believe to be that of Monsieur Armand. I'm afraid there's been an accident, a fatal accident. The car went out of control, came off the road then crashed down the mountainside. There is a body inside and Monsieur Armand's wallet was found on the body."

I wait for a moment to give him time to digest what I've said.

"Do you know if Monsieur Armand had any relatives?" I continue. "Are you aware of his next of kin?"

Falandry clears his throat. "He lives alone in rented accommodation. Perhaps his landlady will know. I could give you her phone number."

"That would be most helpful," I agree.

There is a pause then Falandry asks, "Did you find any papers in the car? Gregory was bringing me information about the death of my wife. He said he'd discovered something interesting about the owner of the spa and the doctor who signed her death certificate. It's imperative I receive Armand's notes."

"I am sorry sir," I say, "But anything found in the car will be held by the police until his next of kin is located. We cannot hand over his belongings to a stranger."

"I was not a stranger to Gregory, he was working for me! Any notes pertaining to my late wife belong to me. I was paying him for the information."

"With respect, sir, you told me he was on his way to see you in order to be paid. At this precise time, you have bought nothing. You have no rights over his notes unless they are in a sealed envelope addressed to you, and under these circumstances, we would post them to you once our investigation is complete."

"This is ridiculous! It's preposterous! I need his notes so I can claim what is rightfully mine. How do you expect me to proceed with my case?"

I am disgusted that Falandry is more interested in his pursuit of money than the death of Gregory Armand.

"Perhaps you should hire another detective and start again," I suggest. "It's a shame Armand let you down. He picked a most inopportune time to die."

I guess Falandry is annoyed by my sarcastic reply because he slams down the phone. I suppose I'll have to try to find Armand's next of kin from the contents of his car. One thing is sure though – I have no intention of giving Falandry any information that will hurt my friend Poullet or my potential business partner, Claude.

The day drags on and I hear nothing more about Armand until almost close of day, when I receive a phone call from Jerome, asking me to stay at the office because he's on his way to see me. He arrives just as we are about to lock the door. He is carrying a briefcase in one hand and a large black bin sack in the other. I tell my men they can go, asking Paul to lock the door as he leaves then I show Jerome through to my office where I put on a pot of coffee. He drops the bin sack onto the floor in the corner of the room and places the briefcase beside it. Then he sits down, leisurely stretching his long legs out in front of him.

"I'm sorry about the sack of rubbish," he says, "But it seems our Monsieur Armand wrote notes on everything so there's cigarette packets and paper bags, even a fast food box from Mc-Donald's. I'm afraid you'll have to plough through the whole grubby mixture and decide what's important and what's not."

I don't care how much rubbish I need to go through, I think – somewhere in that sack or in the briefcase is the information for Falandry.

"Have you been working on the mountain all day?" I ask. "It must have been cold up there."

"Very cold, we've been freezing our *testicule* for seven hours. And what a horrible job it was, recovering the body. We had to cut through the tree branch and part of the car seat and all the while the poor man's eyes were looking up at us from the floor of his car. We couldn't reach the head until we'd recovered the body. Those staring eyes will haunt me. It was ghastly."

"Where's the body now?" I ask.

"Being autopsied, you'll get a report in a few days. The car is in the police garage, we could look at it tomorrow if you'd like."

"How on earth will they carry out the autopsy with a tree branch stuck through the middle of the body?" I say. "I don't fancy the doctor's job."

"Nor do I," Jerome says. "And that's another thing that's bothering me. When we eventually got the corpse into a body bag, we didn't know what to do with the head to stop it from rolling about so we wedged it between the man's legs. We forgot to straighten it out when we put the body in the fridge. So the doctor who's doing the autopsy is going to think we were taking the piss and being disrespectful, when really, we were just being practical."

Quite suddenly, the whole gruesome story seems funny and I begin to smile. Jerome starts to laugh and so do I.

"It brings a whole new meaning to having one's head up one's arse," Jerome says and we giggle helplessly.

Graveyard humour always breaks the tension, but people who don't have to deal with such situations would probably be shocked by our behaviour.

"What time should I meet you at the garage?" I ask when we finally regain some composure.

"I've a call to make first thing," he replies. "How about ten-thirty, does that suit you?"

"Yes, I can make that time. Do I need to bring anything with me?"

"Only a strong stomach – the car's covered in blood. I'll have protective clothing for us. Perhaps we could do lunch afterwards," he adds with a smile, and for the first time I realise just how handsome Jerome is.

"Do you think we'll feel like eating after the job we have to do?"

"If not I'll buy you a liquid lunch," he replies. "We'll certainly need that."

We chat for a few minutes more then I gather up my things and walk Jerome to the door. He hangs about as I lock up and we stand awkwardly, each waiting for the other to leave.

"Until tomorrow," I finally say reaching out to shake his hand.

I'm aware of him clutching my hand for too long and I blush. He smiles and winks at me.

"*À bientôt,*" he replies.

He was flirting with me, I think as I drive home. He was definitely flirting. Patricia and I are friends but we will never be lovers, although we do love each other very much. We are closer than most married couples and rely on each other completely. I always wondered what would happen if one of us met someone, but I never expected I would be the one faced with the dilemma. I know I shouldn't feel guilty, after all, it's only lunch with a colleague, but something about Jerome stirred me. I felt a thrill when he held onto my hand and the prospect of seeing him again makes me both scared and excited all at the same time.

Chapter 22

I carefully apply make-up, not too much, just enough to enhance my looks.

"Hot date?" Patricia jokes. "You don't usually wear make-up to work."

"Actually, I'm meeting a colleague for lunch," I admit. "A fireman from further up the valley."

"Oh, I see," she replies and busies herself at the sink. "Have you known him long?"

"Not really, we met on a job," I reply. "We're looking at Gregory Armand's car this morning then having a bite to eat. No big deal," I add.

"Right," she replies, tidying the kitchen and banging pots and pans as she clears. "By the way, your Mum and Dad are coming for Christmas dinner. Your Dad telephoned and it's all arranged. Byron is bringing them in his car. I phoned him and invited him after we discussed it. I thought I'd go through to Perpignan today with Marjorie and buy a few small gifts. Have you anything special in mind for your parents, or will I choose something?"

"I'd appreciate it if you'd pick up something, you're better at judging that sort of thing than me."

Although we have drifted back into our normal routine and conversation, I'm aware of Patricia being careful. There's a slight stiffness between us and I know she's trying to avoid mentioning my 'date', but is obviously troubled by the prospect. I sit and sip my coffee and eat the breakfast she's made and watch as she carries out all the household chores a wife usually takes responsibility for. All the jobs I don't want to do. I realise then how easily and comfortably we each fulfil our different roles in this household. I naturally take over the traditional roles of a husband, such as mending the chicken shed and bringing in the logs, while Patricia handles the cooking and homemaking. I love this life and I don't like change, but when I think about Jerome I feel an excitement I can't explain. I've never been confused about my sexuality. I am not a lesbian like Patricia, but neither do I have any experience of relationships with men.

As I walk down the path to my car Patricia runs after me. "Wait, Danielle," she calls. She places the Russian hat on my head, careful not to mess up my hair. "You'd better wear this today and take these," she adds handing me my scarf and gloves. "It's freezing. The forecast says the maximum temperature today is only going to be six degrees. You don't want to get a chill." Patricia looks deeply into my eyes. "Enjoy your lunch," she says. "Just be yourself and see what comes of it. You never know, this man might turn out to be a complete bore or the love of your life."

We stand motionless, staring at each other. Her eyes are full of pain and worry.

It's in that single moment I realise that it is Patricia who is the love of my life. Nobody will ever love me as she does. She would sacrifice her happiness for mine. Even though the risk of losing what we have terrifies her, she is still willing to put my needs before her own.

"Don't be daft, darling," I reply. "Compared to you, everyone I meet is a complete bore. From time to time, it's enjoyable to eat oysters or sip a fine brandy, but you wouldn't want to do it every day. Lunch with a handsome stranger is exactly the same. A little taste of something different to let me appreciate all the things I already have and love. You have nothing to worry about, Patricia. You are my future and nothing will ever change that."

She throws her arms around me and hugs me. "I wouldn't stand in your way. You know that, don't you? You're a hetero-sexual woman with needs I can't fulfil. If you want to have a man in your life, I'd understand." Tears run down her cheeks and she swipes them away with her hands.

"Stop being so soppy, woman," I say. "Get back in that kitchen and do your work. If I don't get a move on I'm going to be late."

I physically turn her around and give her a gentle shove to-wards the house. I'm angry at myself. Why did I open my mouth about Jerome? How could I upset her like that? If I do develop any sort of friendship with him, I'll have to be discreet and not risk spoiling what I have or causing any hurt to Patricia.

I arrive at my office before eight o'clock, immediately put on protective gloves and pick up Armand's briefcase. It has some blood spots on it but they've dried, so it's not too bad to handle. I have neither the time nor the inclination to tackle the bin sack now, and depending on what I find in the case, I might not have to give its contents more than a cursory glance. The briefcase is not locked and when I open it, I see it contains two card-board files, one notebook, one address book and a large brown envelope with the name 'Falandry' handwritten on the front, plus the usual pens, pencils, paperclips, etcetera. The envelope is unsealed, so I tip the contents of it onto my desk.

The first thing I see is a sheet of paper with the heading 'Un-expected Deaths by Heart Attack'. There are four names listed and one of these is Madame Falandry. According to the dates, each of the deaths occurred within a two-month period. All the deaths were witnessed by Doctor Poullet and Monsieur Claude, which is strange because Poullet had no reason to be in atten-dance, but even more unusually, they all occurred early morning before the spa was fully open for business. I can't understand why no one has picked up on this information before, until I remember Bertrand Dupont. As I read further, it's clear that each of the people named had a serious medical condition. Two of them had terminal cancer, one suffered from a lung disease and the fourth, poor man, had motor neurone disease. They were all going to die, but probably not from heart attacks.

I lift the next sheet of paper headed 'Gifts and Bequests to Monsieur Claude'. At the top of the list is Madame Falandry's name with a note, saying 'house given to Claude prior to her death'. Then there is the name, Didier Lamont and beside it the figure 14,865 euros, with a note saying 'see solicitors letter'. The next on the list is Madame Emmanuelle Large and written beside her name is 12,086 euros, payment for treatment, then finally, Denis Manet, 18,900 euros, payment for treatment. I find the letter from Didier Lamont's solicitors – it states that he had no known relatives and he bequeathed his estate to Monsieur Claude 'for care, compassion and treatment'. A huge sum of money is involved, I think, how much treatment could each person have had? This is dynamite. No wonder Falandry is desperate to get his hands on it. I must speak with Claude and see what he has to say about it. I hear voices in the outer office, confirming my team has arrived to start work, so I lock the papers in my desk drawer. I don't want anyone else to see what I've discovered.

I'm getting ready to go to the police garage, brushing my hair and touching up my lipstick, when I hear a commotion. When I go into the main office to find out what's going on I see Albert being restrained by Marcel, and Laurent is on his knees picking desk items off the floor.

"He kicked over the bin," Marcel explains.

"And he swept all the stuff that was on my desk onto the floor," Laurent says.

"What's going on here?" I ask Albert. "Why are you acting like this?"

"He's dead! Gregory Armand is dead," Albert whines. "He promised to look into my case. He said he'd take it on a no win, no fee basis, and now he's dead!"

Albert has clearly had a drink or two. Even at this early hour, he's slurring his words.

"And what case would that be?" I ask.

"My parents – they were killed in a car crash you know. Just like Monsieur Armand. Then Michelle, my cousin, cheated me out of my inheritance. She sold the apartment block to Monsieur Claude. Now he wants me out, so he can develop it for use by the 'curists' coming to the spa. Where will I live? Am I to be put out onto the street?"

"Albert," I say gently. "What do you expect me to do? Have you been to see the *notaire*?"

"Pah," he spits, "that crook helped my dear cousin to cheat me. They're all in cahoots, Michelle, Claude and Boutiere! They're a bunch of thieves." He begins to weep and Marcel releases his arm.

"I'm sorry, Albert, but I can't help you," I say. "I can't see how anyone could change what has occurred – not even Gregory Armand. I take it he wanted information from you and gave you the promise of help in order to get you to talk to him. Am I right?"

Albert's cheeks redden and he slaps his hands to his face. "Is everyone a cheat? Is everyone a robber? Am I the brunt of everyone's jokes?" he asks. "The whole town is probably laughing at me. 'Look at stupid Albert', they'll say, 'the fool who has nothing'."

"I think you'd better leave now, Albert. I'm just leaving for a meeting. I'll walk with you."

Marcel opens the door. I grab my bag, grip Albert's elbow and walk him out. I feel rather sorry for him, but he is a stupid man and he can be very nasty when he's drunk, so there won't be many people queuing up to help him. I'm just amazed that

Claude has kept him on, working at the spa – but then again, perhaps he has something to feel guilty about?

Chapter 23

I arrive at the police garage at ten twenty-five. Jerome is already there, suited and booted. He hands me the protective clothing, but when I put it on he doubles up with laughter.

"You look like a kid wearing her Dad's overalls," he says, rolling up the excess fabric at my wrists and ankles. "I guess these coveralls are designed for the men in the fire service."

Jerome gently brushes my hair out of my eyes with his fingers, then seems embarrassed by his actions.

"Sorry," he says and looks away, but not before I notice he's blushing. "You'd better tie your hair back. You don't want to touch it if you have blood on your gloves."

I reach in my bag and fish out a scrunchie. "Is that better?" I ask. "I don't have a mirror. Have I got it all?"

He stares at me for a few moments. "That's perfect," he says.

I find his gaze very flattering. Now I'm the one who's blushing.

"We'd better get started," I say, trying to hide my discomfort. "The sooner we begin the sooner we'll be finished."

"And the sooner we can break for lunch," he adds. "I'll just fetch the mechanic over. The car is by the back wall. You can't miss it. It's the one with the roof cut off." He gives me a wry smile.

The mechanic is thorough. He points out all the things we need to know about the car.

"Look at this," he says, exhaling his breath with a whistle. "There's a little hole in the brake pipe. The brake fluid must have been dripping out for the whole journey, but he probably had no reason to use his brakes very much on the way up the mountain, so it would only be when he was coming back down that he got into trouble. At some point, he's hauled on the hand brake and the engine was switched off at the key. The poor man tried everything to stop the car, but he didn't have a chance."

"Could the car have been deliberately sabotaged?" I ask.

"We'll never know for sure," the mechanic replies. "It's just a small hole. The pipe hasn't been cut. I suppose it is possible, though. Someone who knows about engines could have damaged it, but they couldn't have guessed the speed that the fluid would run out or how long it would take before the brakes were compromised. Do you think somebody was trying to scare the driver?"

"I can't imagine who," I reply. "I think, if we're all agreed, this should be written down as a tragic accident."

The two men nod in agreement.

"Are we done then?" Jerome asks. He looks at his watch. "By the time we get cleaned up and get to the restaurant, it will be time for lunch. I'm starving, how about you?"

Surprisingly, I do feel rather hungry. I rose very early this morning and I haven't had much to eat.

"Where are we eating?" I ask. "Is it nearby?"

"I thought the *salon de the* in the town centre. They do a very good lunch of quiche with a mixed salad and they have wonderful desserts. They also sell hand-made chocolates," he adds.

"So not a burger and fries, then?" I joke.

"I'm sorry, I thought being a girl, you'd like something a bit more refined, but if I've got it wrong..."

"I'm teasing you," I reply. "Your choice sounds great."

I start to peel off the protective suit and once again, Jerome blushes. He stares at the ground and rubs an imaginary spot with his foot. "Your shirt buttons have opened," he says, "When you pulled your arm out of the sleeve."

I quickly pull my shirt closed and redo the buttons. He was watching me as I took off the suit, I think. Otherwise, he wouldn't have noticed my shirt. I find myself both flattered and unnerved.

The restaurant is only a few minutes away and we are soon seated. It is comfortable and warm and the owner is friendly and attentive without being overbearing. She brings us a jug of water and a basket of fresh bread.

"Would you like some wine with your food?" she asks. "I can recommend the *Corbiere* but the house red is also good, if you'd just like a glass."

"We are both working," Jerome says. "But I don't suppose one glass would do any harm. What do you think, Danielle? Will you have some?"

I wouldn't think twice about having a glass of wine with my lunch, but I don't want him to think badly of me. "Just one then," I agree. "It can't hurt."

We eat the superb food, drink the robust wine and chat like old friends. The time passes quickly. Jerome is such easy company and I am feeling very relaxed when he says, "We'll have to do this again sometime. How are you fixed next week, can we meet up?"

My immediate instinct is to say yes, but I get a flash of Patricia's sweet face in my mind's eye and I hesitate.

Jerome picks up on my hesitation and says, "I'm sorry, I've been too presumptuous; forget I mentioned it."

"I enjoy your company, Jerome," I respond, "but I don't usually mix business with pleasure and I'm not sure that I can. Could you give me some time to think about it, please? Forgive me if I'm wrong, but I feel you're offering me more than just a lunch."

"I really like you, Danielle. You're smart and funny and very pretty and you're right, I was looking for more than just lunch. I'd like to get to know you better. Take all the time you want to decide, no pressure. As long as you eventually say yes," he replies, laughing.

We finally agree to keep in touch and Jerome pays the bill. "My expenses will cover this," he explains.

I know I haven't done anything wrong. I've simply had lunch with a friend, but something is making me feel guilty nevertheless, so I stop at the florist and buy Patricia a bunch of roses before I head back to town. Then I remember that in every trashy romance novel I've ever read, the errant husband always buys flowers for his betrayed wife and a wave of guilt passes over me once again.

Chapter 24

We are only ten days away from Christmas and everything has either stopped or is winding down. Many businesses close for four to six weeks, and apart from the odd tourist driving up the mountain to the ski resorts, there are no strangers even passing through town. It is cold, bitterly cold, the *tremontane* – the wind from the three mountains – cuts through you like a knife. Even when the sun is high and the day is clear, you need to wear a coat. Overnight, Christmas trees which are sprayed white and decorated with brightly packaged boxes have appeared in the main streets, tied to lamp-posts. They look festive when the sun is up, but give the town an eerie, deathly feel at twilight when people are indoors and the street is empty.

My household is no different from the rest; it too is slowing down. There are no pots of jams or preserves bubbling on the stove, no paintings being worked on, the easel is packed away. Patricia is well prepared for the holidays, and apart from tending to the chickens and rabbits, she spends her days pottering about the house or reading. I have completed all the outside repairs and I've gathered a substantial pile of logs for the fire. Our freezer and our larder are full and we could survive a siege if we needed to.

The file on Bertrand Dupont is open, but I'm not being pressed for a result. Detective Gerard hasn't even followed up on the case by email. He's not interested in a death that could very well have been accidental. Everything and everyone in town is grinding to a halt. I feel as if I'm seeing the world in slow motion, yet my mind is racing and I want answers. I'm drowning under a heap of different things I need to deal with. I'm stressed and bad tempered while my colleagues are relaxed and having fun – they're like children excitedly waiting for Santa Claus. Their stupid jokes and banter are irritating me and I'm constantly sending them out of the office to do their shopping or have extra time off, just so I can get some peace. All the information I've gathered is spinning around in my head and I can't put it in any logical order. Everything seems, in some way, interconnected – but I can't work out how.

Adding to this turmoil is Jerome. I can't get him out of my mind. I daydream about him and it's tearing me apart. I don't know how to handle my feelings. I'm like a naïve teenager. I still remember how gentle his fingers felt on my skin as he brushed the hair from my face and I can picture the shy way he dropped his chin then looked up into my eyes when he smiled. I want to be in his company again, but how can I be? How can I betray Patricia? I'm so mixed up. The office walls seem to be closing in on me and I can stand being confined no longer.

"I'm going out," I announce, interrupting yet more daft be-haviour from my colleagues. "Mind the shop."

They don't stop what they're doing. They don't even look at me as I walk out of the door. When I step into the street, I inhale deeply and the icy air hurts my lungs, but I want to feel the cold and I want to feel the pain. I want to punish myself for the thoughts I can't control. Everything is confusing me, in my work and in my personal life. I no longer feel in charge and I hate all the uncertainty I'm experiencing.

I decide to walk to the café, hoping and praying that Byron is sitting in his usual seat by the doorway. I need to talk to some-one and he's the only person I can trust to keep what I say private. I take the long way around, circumnavigating the town, planning what I want to discuss with him. As I make my way up the hill towards the spa, I see it. Spray-painted in red letters, a metre high, emblazoned on the front of the building, the word *voleur* – thief. Merde, I think to myself, this is all I need. I have my phone in my hand and I'm about to call the office when it rings.

"You'd better come back here, Boss," Paul says when I answer it. "Madame Moliner and Monsieur Boutiere have just arrived and they're raging. Something about spray paint."

First the spa, now the estate agent and the *notaire* – there can only be one culprit. "Oh, Albert, what have you done, you stupid man?" I mutter to myself. "Now you'll really be in the shit."

"I'm on my way, Paul," I reply. "Send Laurent to go and pick up Albert. He'll probably be drunk, so I don't want him put into one of the cars in case he throws up. In fact, you'd better send Marcel as well. It might take them both to drag him in. Tell Michelle and Pascal that I'll be with them as soon as possible. They can wait for me if they want, or you can take their statements."

"Okay, Boss," Paul replies. In a quiet voice, he adds, "They're absolutely livid. Madame Moliner is pacing the floor like a caged animal. I'll do my best, but I don't think they'll leave until they can speak to you."

I'm glad I keep a bottle of brandy in my desk drawer, because I think I'm going to need it. Michelle Moliner is bad-tempered at the best of times, and this will not be the best of times.

* * *

As I approach the office I see Michelle through the window. She is still pacing. Her narrow, pinched, rat-like face is white with rage and she's waving her hands in the air as she complains to poor Paul. He has placed himself behind a desk, keeping her at arm's length, and I don't blame him. She looks mad enough to bite. Boutiere is sitting with his head in his hands; he looks weary. I open the door and they all turn towards me.

"Bonjour, Monsieur-Damme," I say, running the words together as is the custom. "You'd better come into my office." I don't offer them coffee and before Michelle can go off on another rant I continue. "I know why you're here. There's spray paint at the spa as well. My men are picking up Albert as we speak. I'm sure we'll discover that he's the culprit, and when we prove it, he will be charged. All that remains is for you both to give statements to my colleague. Then may I suggest you return to your offices and try to find a tradesman to remove the offensive words before all the businesses close for the holidays. Otherwise, the paint could be there until the middle of January."

Michelle looks as if she's going to say something, but Pascal rises from his chair.

"Danielle's absolutely right. We'd better get going and try to find someone who can remove the paint before the rest of the town sees it." He turns to me. "Albert painted the word *menteur*, liar, across my windows and the word '*voleur*' across the front of Michelle's shop. How dare he? Who does he think he is? I am a public official under the authority of the Minister of Justice. I make my living upholding the law and telling the truth."

I notice he's not protesting Michelle's position.

"Albert's a drunk, a bitter, twisted drunk and he'll pay for what he's done," Michelle says. "I've tried to help him. I even put a roof over his head when his parents died, but not any more. He can fend for himself. I wipe my hands of him."

I know she has contrived with Monsieur Claude to turf Albert out of his apartment and she probably did steal his inheritance in the first place. I don't like the woman and I'm not too keen on Claude or Boutiere either, but they are wealthy, influential people, and if I'm forced to take sides, I would choose them over the town drunk any day of the week.

Chapter 25

I am unable to discover the next of kin of Gregory Armand. We have contacted every name in his address book, but no one listed there was related to him. They were all clients, or people he had business dealings with. The notebook and the bin sack revealed nothing either. I have no option but to hand everything over to the central office in Perpignan. It's their problem now. I have, however, retained the contents of the envelope. It's best if I alone know of its existence. I can't have strangers snooping around my town.

Laurent and Marcel eventually find Albert, sitting on a boulder by the riverside. I am told that he was still clutching a can of spray paint, which he wielded like a weapon when they tried to speak to him, managing to spray Laurent's shoes and trousers. I am further informed that on trying to apprehend him, Marcel was pushed into the river. So after calling for a van from Ceret to collect Albert, both men needed to go home to get changed. Honestly, they are like 'Laurel and Hardy'. Comical disasters keep happening to them, except they're not trying to be funny. Thank goodness I have Paul. At least I have one useful officer on my team.

The day is quiet, nobody has walked through the door since Michelle and Pascal left the office and the phone has hardly rung, so I'm confident that Paul can manage on his own until the others return.

"Have you brought your lunch with you today?" I ask him.

"Yes, Boss, I was hoping to work through the break and get off early if that's okay. I've got some shopping to do in Perpignan."

"No problem, Paul," I reply. "I'll go out just now as I have a couple of things to attend to. Will you manage on your own until those dimwits return?"

"I'll manage better on my own. Trust me, Boss, much better."

I gather up my bag and leave. Although I'm sure Byron won't be at the café now, I make my way over there just in case. As I approach, I see that seated at Byron's usual table are Monsieur Claude and Madame Moliner. I glance around for somewhere to duck out of view, but I'm too late – Claude has spotted me.

"Danielle, Danielle, over here," he calls, beckoning to me. When I walk over to him, he says, "I'm glad you're here. I was just saying to Michelle that I wanted to have a word with you."

"Have you apprehended Albert yet?" Michelle asks, her voice sharp and her lips pinched. I suspect if she smiled her face would crack.

"Yes," I reply. "He still had a can of paint gripped in his hand. He was very drunk so he must have been drinking all night long. My men sent him to Ceret to be charged, but they'll release him when he sobers up."

"Typical," Claude says. "I know the spa is closed for the season, but he leaves me no option. I'm going to terminate his employment. How dare he say I'm a thief and how dare he damage my property? I want to be rid of him completely. I want him out of my apartment building too."

"You can't evict him in winter. It's the law," Michelle says. "You'll just have to be patient, but at least if he's unemployed, social housing money will be paid directly to you so he can't spend his days drinking it, and more importantly, he'll no longer be living rent free in your property."

"Yes, I have you to thank for allowing him that arrangement, Michelle. The responsibility was passed to me when I bought the building from you, but he's not my cousin, I owe him nothing. He can pay the damned rent like everyone else. I was doing you the favour, not him."

Michelle looks at her watch. "I'm sorry," she says, "But I have to go. Let me know what happens with Albert," she adds, addressing me.

Michelle plants the customary kisses on my cheeks. Her narrow rat-like features unnerve me. I always think she might bite my face with her little sharp teeth. Claude orders me a coffee then takes a folder of papers from a bag at his feet.

"These are the plans for my building," he explains. "The business proposal we briefly talked about." He spreads the paperwork onto the table. "As you can see, the building is substantial. At the moment, there are fifteen apartments but with a fairly simple redesign there could be twenty-six luxury, ensuite studios. Each studio could be rented to 'curists', bringing in an income of a thousand euros a month for about eleven months of the year. The return is astonishing, don't you agree?"

"Absolutely," I reply. "But what does this have to do with me?"

"When Albert's parents were alive, his father tried to have this building converted once before. The main opposition to his proposal came from the police. There is no parking and no easy access for fire services to the rear of the building, although it's the same situation currently. Some police official in Perpignan, who had never been to our town or seen the building, felt that by increasing the number of units, the risk would increase, but that's nonsense. With you now in charge of the police here, it is you who would be on the panel to decide whether permission should be granted."

"And you want me to vote in favour of the reconstruction?"

"Precisely."

"The works are going to take a lot of money, but you seem to have inherited several large sums recently. That is very fortuitous."

Monsieur Claude blushes. "Ah yes," he replies making no attempt to deny this, "Very."

"You mentioned a business proposition. What do you expect of me?" I ask.

"I will gift you a ten percent stake in the building and the same cut of the annual profit for your support and help with the planning application. It will cost you nothing and you won't have to do any of the work. Pascal Boutiere will draw up the paperwork and you can take it away and have it checked out by any solicitor or *notaire* of your choosing. The income will be constant as the spa will provide the renters. It can't lose."

The opportunity is huge. It takes me only seconds to calculate the value of his offer.

"When do I have to decide?" I ask.

"After the Christmas holidays will be soon enough. As Michelle rightly pointed out, I can't evict Albert during the winter months." Claude gathers up his papers then gets to his feet. "I'm sorry but I have to get going now, my wife is expecting me to drive her to Perpignan so she can shop. I hate this time of year. I seem to spend so much time driving around all over the place, achieving very little and parking is a nightmare."

I want to discuss the spate of recent deaths from heart attack at the spa with Claude, and the large amounts of money he's been gifted, but I don't think the timing is right. His offer has given me something more important to think about.

Chapter 26

A very contrite Albert arrives in the office the next day. His face is chalk-white and puffy, and dark grey hollows surround his bloodshot eyes.

"I've come to apologise," he says. He can't look any of us in the eye. "I've been a fool, a complete idiot. I was out of my head with alcohol and I know it's no excuse, but I was upset, absolutely distraught."

We are all staring at him, but no one says a word. We get so many drunks apologising after their appalling behaviour that we're fed up hearing it.

"Gregory's death reminded me, you see," he continues. "It took me right back to the time when I lost my parents. They were killed when their car went out of control."

I sigh, I've heard all this before, even though the event occurred outside my jurisdiction.

"Everyone thought my Papa was drunk, but he wasn't, the blood test proved that," Albert continues. "He was run off the road by another vehicle. There were long scrapes and bumps the whole length of his car. His vehicle was silver, but the scrapes had blue paint on them. The blood test results took three weeks to come back because the first batch were lost and by that time, everyone had pretty much made up their minds. He liked a drink you see. Just like me, but he wasn't drunk all the time and he didn't even drink every day."

This is news to me. I'd never heard this version of the story before, but then I've been told about Albert's parents by Michelle Moliner.

"Michelle told everyone a complete lie, and because she's well known and has influence in town, that's the story they believed. She and Boutiere concocted some kind of deal. She said my Papa owed her a lot of money and Boutiere had some paperwork that seemed to prove it. The court believed her and awarded her Papa's property as payment. With the help of that liar, she stole my inheritance. Gregory said he'd look into it for me. That's why I showed him the files in Monsieur Claude's office. It was my way of paying for his time. Now he's dead and I have nothing."

We let him ramble on. Paul is working at his computer and Laurent is sorting the filing on his desk. Marcel silently leaves the office to buy the *pain-au-raisins* for the morning break. Only I continue to give him my full attention.

"I've been fired, you know?" he says. "Claude has given me notice. I'm taking care of the spa over the holidays, but when it re-opens in February, I'll be discharged."

"I'm sorry, Albert," I say, "Claude did tell me of his intentions."

"He's trying to get me out of my flat too, but he can't do that until the winter is over. I swear to you, Danielle, if I end up on the street with nothing but a bag of my belongings, I'll kill Claude, you mark my words. I'll kill him and Michelle."

"You'd better stop right there, Albert," I warn. "If I hear you making threats like that I'll have to arrest you. No matter how upset you are, and I can understand how you feel, you cannot make death threats."

He hangs his head; the effort of speaking has exhausted him.

"I'm going home," he states. "While I still have a home to go to, but Claude won't get rid of me as easily as he thinks. I know things. I know what he's been up to. I don't need Gregory. I can work things out for myself."

"Just don't go making accusations you can't back up," I warn. "And no more threats or damaging property. You're in enough trouble already."

Albert purses his lips, he's annoyed at me and he turns and marches out, trying to slam the door behind him, but it's on a spring so it closes in its own sweet time no matter how hard it's pulled or pushed. The irony of him failing once again is not lost on me. It seems that on every level, this sad character just can't win.

I assume Albert gave Gregory Armand access to the information about the deaths from heart attacks and the bequests. He has keys to the building and it would have been easy for him to have borrowed Claude's desk key and have it copied. He could have done it months or even years ago.

I need to speak to my old friend Poullet, because I know he's involved. I need to be sure that each case can stand up to investigation. I need to know that Poullet has done nothing wrong. I haven't seen or heard anything from the good doctor since the death of Bertrand Dupont, even though I've left several messages. He's avoiding me, but he can't hide for ever and I can't wait any longer for answers. If I'm to keep all the balls in the air, I need to know what I'm up against.

I don't want my deal with Claude to be put at risk. I want a share of that building and a share of the income, but I must be seen to be whiter than white especially if I'm to be instrumental in granting the planning permission. I'll also have to figure out a way of receiving my cut whilst not being seen to be connected to it. Claude will have to tread very carefully where Albert is concerned. The man is trouble, he's like a ticking bomb and Claude needs to find a way of defusing the situation.

Chapter 27

I'm dying to tell Patricia about the deal Claude has offered. The regular money from rentals could give us an added income for life. We're not short of money and I'll receive a good pension, but how many people of our age would ever be given a chance like this? After parking badly, I race up the path and open the front door, but before I even cross the threshold Patricia is beside me, talking ten to the dozen, imparting her exciting news. Ollee is getting in on the act by leaping up and aiming licks at my face, bumping me with his wet nose.

"Gilbert and Stuart are being married in January in Glasgow, and of course, we're invited," she says breathlessly. "They've booked a stately home for the reception and all the men are going to wear kilts. They've managed to get a cancellation, that's why it's happening so soon. January the twenty-fifth. It's a Friday. Oh, and Marjorie says there's to be a Scottish country dance called a ceilidh after the dinner. She's arranging for a Scottish lady to come to our dance class so we can learn some of the steps. Sarah said she'd look after Ollee and Mimi and the hens and rabbits. We can go, can't we? You'll be able to get time off, won't you? January is always a quiet month."

I manage to hold Ollee still while I wriggle out of my coat. Patricia unpeels my scarf and places my shoulder bag on a chair. I still haven't managed to say a word before she begins again.

"Sorry, Danielle, I'm going on and on, but I'm so excited. We've only ever been abroad once before when we went to London. Do you think people wear kilts all the time in Scotland? Perhaps we'll have to eat haggis for our dinner. I'm not sure I fancy that. Speaking of dinner, ours is ready; go and get changed and I'll serve it, you must be famished."

She disappears over to the stove with Ollee in hot pursuit. Dinner is one word he understands. I guess my news will have to wait.

We are halfway through our roast chicken before Patricia is all talked out. We've agreed that yes, we will go to Glasgow and, yes, we will attend the wedding and yes, we will get Sarah to watch the animals. As it turns out, Marjorie is going to book our flights and our hotel when she makes the bookings for her family. All we'll have to do is get ourselves to Barcelona airport on time to fly out. It seems we can't travel from Perpignan or Girona, even though both are much closer, because there are no flights in or out of either airport connecting to anywhere in Scotland.

Finally, it's my turn to speak.

"I've been offered a business deal," I say. "A fantastic opportunity that's worth a lot of money, but I've got to figure out a way of accepting it."

I explain the offer and my dilemma. It can't look as if I'm accepting a bribe. If anything goes wrong I must be able to walk away.

Patricia sits quietly, thinking about what I've told her. "I have the perfect solution. Monsieur Claude can hire me as a designer! I am an artist and a businesswoman after all. I'll open a new interior design company and a new business bank account. Claude can pay my company with a share of the building and a percentage of the income. Then you're not involved at all. It will be a legitimate business transaction with Claude hiring me in the same way he'll hire the builders to do the remodelling. I'll create a file with drawings of interiors and samples of fabrics and lists of supply companies. I'll tell people I'm working on the project, lots of people, so there's no doubt it's me and not you who's involved. What do you think? Will that work?"

I rise from my chair, go over to Patricia, cup her face in my hands and plant a kiss on her forehead.

"Do I tell you often enough that you're a genius?" I ask. "Because I don't think I do."

She laughs and punches me playfully in the ribs and I release her face. "Of course I'm a genius," she says. "That's why you love me."

Suddenly, I get an image of Jerome in my mind's eye and I feel awful. Why am I thinking of him when I have everything and everyone I need here? I don't want him to complicate my life. I don't want things to change, but I can't get the image of his face out of my head.

Chapter 28

I finally track down Poullet at his house and when I ring the doorbell, it is he who opens the door.

"Danielle," he says by way of a greeting, but he doesn't step aside or invite me in.

"I need to speak to you about Madame Falandry. May I come in?" I ask.

"Have you not been to my office?" he replies shortly. "Did you not see the sign saying I'm on holiday? Can't this wait?" He still blocks the doorway.

"I also wish to discuss Monsieur Didier Lamont, Monsieur Denis Manet and Madame Emmanuelle Large," I add.

He stares hard into my eyes. I return his gaze, unflinching.

"You'd better come in," he finally agrees and he steps aside to let me enter. When we are seated in his study he asks, "How did you find out?"

"Gregory Armand," I answer.

"But the man is dead," Poullet says.

"Yes, but I have his notes."

We sit in silence for a minute then Poullet asks, "What are you going to do, Danielle? Am I to be arrested like a common criminal?"

I have no idea what he's talking about, but Poullet seems to think that I know something.

"Why don't you start at the beginning and tell me your version of events," I suggest. "Then we can decide what to do about the situation."

He sighs. "Very well." He lifts a bottle of brandy and two glasses from the cabinet beside him, placing them on the desk between us. Poullet sits, lifts the bottle, opens it and pours some of the golden liquid into each glass. He hasn't asked if I want some – he just assumes that I'll need it and that's worrying.

"All of the people you've mentioned had terminal illnesses," he begins. "They were all suffering from terrible pain and fear. It began with Didier Lamont. The poor man had become incontinent and the loss of his dignity horrified him. I met him quite by chance when I visited the spa to deliver a package to my wife's friend, Madame Georges. He was sitting on a bench at the entranceway, crying. He was all alone and I stopped to ask him if he was all right. Normally, I would have walked past; I wouldn't have engaged him in conversation, but something about the way Monsieur Lamont looked reminded me of my late father, so I stopped." Poullet sips at his brandy. "He had no family, you see," he continues, "No one to look after him or to care if he lived or died. He'd read of the spa on the social network site, 'Facebook'. Someone had written about their miracle cure after visiting for treatment and Didier would have gone anywhere or tried anything for a chance to improve his health."

"But he didn't die from his illness, did he?" I comment. "He died of a heart attack that you and Claude witnessed."

"Yes, yes, Danielle," Poullet snaps. "I'm getting to that. I'm just trying to explain to you what happened. Have you no patience?"

Feeling chastised, I sip the brandy and wait for him to continue.

"You have to understand that as a doctor, it's in my nature, my very being, to want to help people and make them well. When they are suffering, I want to end their pain."

A cold chill run down my spine. I have a horrible feeling that I know where this is going.

"After our first encounter, I met with Didier another few times. I liked the man. He even visited this house on one occasion, with Claude. We all had a passion for classic cars you see. Didier once owned a Citröen DS."

Poullet takes a handkerchief from his pocket and wipes his brow. It's not hot in the room, but he's sweating profusely.

"Didier was coming to the end of his treatment at the spa when we hatched our plan to help him. It took several weeks for us to arrange things, as Didier had to see to his affairs before returning here. I didn't know that during that time, he got in touch with several other desperately ill people. They became part of a very small, elite circle; all of them terminally ill and all of them alone in the world – except for Madame Falandry, of course, who lied about her circumstances. Once we'd helped Didier, we had to help the others because they knew, you see – they knew what we had done and there was no going back."

"You killed them," I state, and I can hardly believe I'm saying the words. "You and Claude killed them all. How? How did you do it?"

"I euthanized them. I didn't murder them. They wanted to die and I enabled them to do so painlessly. We give our beloved pets a chance to die with dignity, yet we torture people until their last gram of strength has gone and their bodies are pain-wracked shells."

I am shocked to my very core. Poullet doesn't think he's done anything wrong. He has put four people to death yet he feels no remorse.

"Did they pay you to end their lives? Was there some kind of arrangement?"

"No, Danielle, no of course not!" he protests. "I'm not a monster. I just wanted to help them to end their suffering. No money changed hands. They paid the spa for their treatment and included a little for their funerals, that's all. I received nothing. How could you think that of me? You know me better than that, surely, Danielle?"

I believe Poullet. He has no idea that Claude has accepted vast sums of money from these people and I'm not going to enlighten him.

"Is there anyone else waiting to die?" I ask. "Have any other arrangements been made?"

"There was one more person, but she died last week, before she could travel here."

"I know you say there were no relatives, but surely they had friends or a priest who would miss them. Why did no one come looking for them?"

"They were a very select group," Poullet replies. "They were all members of the Humanist Society. It's a mostly atheistic group, so no religion – therefore, no priests involved. They settled all their affairs before they came here, disposed of their property, left instructions with lawyers, closed their bank accounts, and in Madame Large's case, re-homed her cat. If Madame Falandry hadn't lied to us, everything would have been all right. Nobody would ever have questioned the deaths."

"But Bertrand Dupont wasn't happy," I say. "He thought something was wrong. He mentioned it to his wife. He wanted to talk to Claude about it. Then he was murdered." I pause. "You and Claude, you didn't..." My words trail off. I can't believe I'm thinking these thoughts.

"Of course not!" he exclaims. "What do you take me for? I told you, I'm not a murderer. I helped these people, they were grateful to me. Bertrand Dupont was not a good person. He used to beat his wife. He wouldn't have cared about these strangers, unless perhaps, he thought he could gain something from his knowledge. Claude hasn't mentioned anything to me about Dupont, so I'm quite sure he didn't speak to him about this. Perhaps Bertrand shared his thoughts with someone other than his wife, someone dangerous."

"Do you have anyone in mind?" I ask. "Has anyone approached you?"

"Only Gregory Armand and now you," he replies. "What do we do?" he asks. "Will you arrest me and Claude? Am I to be charged?"

I'm not sure what to do. "Let me think about this for a moment," I say and we sit in silence, sipping our brandies. "If someone were to exhume the bodies and do an autopsy, what would they discover?" I ask. "Would they know you had euthanized these people?"

"The bodies were all cremated, so there's nothing to autopsy."

"That explains why Madame Falandry's ashes were interred in her family crypt, instead of her body. You could have slipped up there, Poullet. Her husband is still looking for answers."

He rubs his brow with his fingers. "What can I do?" he asks. "Has the husband any evidence? Did Armand give him any information?"

"Armand would have given Falandry everything he needed to expose you and Claude if he hadn't crashed on the mountain. I have his notes and his letter to Falandry. They were recovered from the wreck. Don't worry, no one else has seen them. Or ever will," I add.

"So you're going to help me?" he questions, relief washing over his face.

"Yes, I'll destroy the paperwork. The only risk I can see is from the unknown person or persons who killed Dupont. They are still out there, and we don't know what information they may have or if they'll try to use it."

"I'll speak to Claude," he says.

"No, I'll speak to Claude," I warn. "You remain on holiday and do nothing. I'll take care of this, but nobody must know we've had this conversation, understand? The euthanasia must cease.

I don't want to hear about any more deaths. Once I destroy the papers we'll close the book on this whole sorry mess, agreed?"

"Certainly, of course, Danielle, I'll never forget what you're doing for me. You can ask anything of me and I'll help you, any time."

I remember Byron and his troubles with his elderly aunt. My parents are not getting any younger and there might come a time when I'll have to call on the services of Doctor Poullet. There might come a time when a dignified end is what I'll want for them. I tuck that thought away for now. Poullet provided his services for free to end pain and suffering. Claude, on the other hand, received vast sums of money and feels no remorse. I think Claude and I need to have another little chat about his business proposition. I think he'll need to rethink his figures.

As I walk away from Poullet's home, my mind is racing. It's taken me a while to absorb the significance of what has occurred as it's difficult to get my head around what he's told me. At first I was sucked in to thinking of his deeds as being kind and benevolent, but now that I'm out of his company and can think clearly, I see them for what they really are. I can't believe he's ended the lives of four people and worse, he doesn't think he's done anything wrong. It's so shocking, I can't take it in. Poullet is precise in everything he does and he never breaks the rules, although on occasion, he has been known to bend them. He's smart, honest and decent, or so I thought. I respect the man enormously. He's helped me further my career. Poullet can be a grumpy, cantankerous old devil, but I can't visualise him as a murderer, never a murderer, and yet I know now that he is. I've said I'll protect him and I'll try to keep my word.

I sincerely hope Falandry gives up on his search now that Armand has gone and I've got to make sure that no damning information is left lying in wait at the spa. Whatever Albert found in Claude's desk has to be destroyed and his apartment will have to be searched, in case he's made copies of vital documents. Now, more than ever, I want to be able to prove who killed Bertrand Dupont because I need to know the calibre of the person I'm up against. No one must ever find out what Poullet and Claude have done. I intend to cover up their crimes, but one thing is sure, it will cost them. One way or another, they'll pay for my silence.

Icy rain is beginning to fall. Great cleansing drops hit my face and while others duck their heads and run for shelter, I turn my face upwards to the heavens and let the rain run down my forehead and into my eyes. I walk and walk until my coat is heavy with water and I'm soaked through. Finding myself at the riverbank, I sit on a bench as the sky blackens, the wind blows up and the shower turns into a full-blown storm. There is no one around. Everyone has sensibly gone indoors. The secrets I'm carrying weigh heavily on my conscience, making me feel unclean and isolated. I must choose between either betraying my friend or covering up his crime and thereby betraying my promise to uphold the law. Neither choice sits comfortably with me. I'd like to speak to Patricia, but I've already decided not to tell her about Doctor Poullet because I don't want to upset her. Besides I wouldn't know what to say as Poullet is her physician and she trusts him. It's all such a mess. Quite unexpectedly, I find myself crying. The tears feel hot against my frozen cheeks. I thought I was tough and in control and on the surface I am, but inside I'm quaking. I wish my life could return to being simple and I wish I didn't feel so alone.

I have no idea how long I've sat here, but I'm very cold and shivery and wet right through to my skin, even my underwear is soaked. It's time to move. The river is surging and the force of it is making the bridge vibrate; the storm is gaining momentum. I want to go home. Surely no one will call at the office in this weather? With cold, numb fingers I take out my phone and call Paul to inform him that I won't be back in today and he's to lock up.

"Are you okay, Boss?" he asks with concern. "Your voice is trembling, are you unwell?"

"I'm fine, just cold and wet," I reply. "Close up early and you boys get off home. The weather is getting worse. If anyone is daft enough to go out in this and gets into trouble, dispatch can phone us. I'll see you tomorrow."

I hang up without waiting for the usual pleasantries. All I want to do is get back to the comfort and safety of my home and into a warm bath, but when I do arrive back at the house I find Patricia about to run upstairs with a bucket.

"Something blew into the roof," she says. "I think it was a branch. It's smashed a tile and some water is dripping in at the corner of my room," she explains. "Good grief, what happened to you? You're soaked through! You look as if you've been for a swim. If you peel off those wet clothes, I'll run you a hot bath once I place this bucket upstairs."

"I have a better idea," I reply. "As I'm already wet, I'll go and nail a new tile onto the roof while you make me something to eat and pour me a coffee. It'll only take a couple of minutes. I've got some spare tiles in the shed. Then you can forget about the bucket."

"Isn't it a bit dangerous, Danielle? It's awfully windy."

"Don't worry," I reply. "I know that roof like the back of my hand. I could fix a tile in place with my eyes shut."

Before she can protest any further, I go back outside and set about the task. It takes me longer than I expected, because my hands are so cold and numb and there are two tiles broken. Fortunately, they are at the edge of the roof and can be reached from the ladder, which is just as well because climbing onto a wet roof in these conditions would be foolhardy. I soon have the job done and I feel great satisfaction in completing it. The success is reassuring, it makes me feel strong again and renews the confidence of my convictions.

Chapter 29

When I rise in the morning, there isn't a cloud in the sky and the day is cold, crisp and bright. I go downstairs to retrieve my uniform, which was left to dry on the clothes horse in front of the fire last night. Fortunately, it's dry but my wool coat is still very damp. I'll just have to wear my 'Regatta' jacket. It's waterproof and warm enough, but it doesn't offer my legs any protection from the wind.

"Coffee?" Patricia calls from the kitchen and I jump. I didn't hear her, and Ollee didn't greet me, so assumed I was alone and he was in his usual place in her bedroom. "Sorry," she says. "Ollee's in the garden. The rabbits are slower at this time of year, so he's chasing them with renewed hope," she explains. "He really thinks he can catch one."

We sit down together to have breakfast and I'm pleased to have the opportunity of chatting to her before I leave for work.

"I have an idea about this potential deal with Monsieur Claude," I begin. "How would you feel if the interior design business was real and you were actually paid for your advice and planning?"

"You mean if I really hired the tradesmen and chose the fixtures and fittings?"

"Yes."

"And I'd be paid for my work?"

"Absolutely," I reply.

"I'd love it. It would let me use my brain instead of just my cooking skills. It's something I've always fancied getting involved in. Do you remember when I helped Marjorie design her new bathroom? She was delighted with it, and I saved her money."

I had forgotten about that, but Patricia's right. She did do a very good job then.

"I plan to put a proposal to Claude today, but I had to be sure you'd agree," I explain. "I'll call you later to let you know how I get on."

"This is so exciting," she replies rubbing her hands together. "We could make serious money out of this and have a share in the project as well!"

I rise from the table and kiss her goodbye. As I leave the house, I see Ollee running in circles around and around the garden, chasing his own tail.

"No rabbits, Ollee?" I call to him. "Never mind, your tail's probably easier to catch."

At the mention of his name, he runs at me full tilt and leaps at my face, aiming his tongue at my cheek.

"Down, down, you idiot!" I grumble. "You'll get mud on my clothes." And I hold my hand flat above his head as a deterrent. The dog gives an excited 'yip' then takes off once again, chasing his imaginary prey and I jump into the car before he has a chance to launch himself at me again. I telephone Monsieur Claude from my mobile and arrange to meet him in the café in an hour's time for a chat. Then I call Paul and advise him that I won't be in the office until lunchtime. After the day I had yesterday, I plan to take things easier today.

I park at the office but I don't go in, instead I make my way to the café, intending to have a coffee before Claude arrives. As I approach I see Michelle Moliner sitting at a table near the door, smoking a foul-smelling cigarette. Albert is at an adjacent table, holding his head in his hands. When she sees me, she beckons me to come over.

"Danielle, Danielle, over here!" she calls. "Come and join me."

She attempts a smile, but her face hardly moves as if it's been frozen, wrinkle-free, with Botox.

"How are you, Danielle?" she asks, but doesn't wait for my reply. "I've been chatting to Claude. He tells me you're joining our little band of entrepreneurs. I'm delighted for you." She flashes her sharp little teeth.

"I have no idea what you're talking about," I answer loudly, glancing around to see if anyone has overheard her. "I have no business dealings with Monsieur Claude. Whatever made you think that?"

She realises immediately that I'm angry. "My mistake," she says. "I'm sorry. I misunderstood something he said. Please, forgive me."

I've noticed that Albert is paying attention, and I wonder how much he's heard.

"I have to go," Michelle says, rising. "As I said, I'm sorry for any misunderstanding."

"Michelle, Michelle, we need to talk," Albert calls. He comes over to our table.

"I've told you already, Albert, I don't care about your job and I don't care about your apartment," she snaps. "I've helped you all I can. You got yourself into the mess and you can get yourself out of it. I have no apartments to rent to you, not a single one available for someone on social housing benefit."

"But Michelle," he begs, "You're my cousin. Please don't let me be turned out onto the street."

"Look, there's nothing more I can do for you," she replies. "Please leave me alone." She gives me an exasperated look. "This is what I have to contend with, this constant harassment. I'm exhausted by him."

She speaks about Albert as if he's not there, and I'm embarrassed for him.

"Why don't you go and register for the hostel in Ceret. At least you'd have a roof over your head and who knows, you might make friends with other homeless, jobless losers like yourself," she finishes cruelly.

Albert hangs his head. Michelle plants kisses on my cheeks, drops a five euro note on the table to cover the cost of her coffees, and walks off without a backward glance.

"Don't get involved with her," Albert warns. "She's a bitch; a lying, thieving bitch and I hate her with all my heart. She wouldn't piss on me if I was on fire, she's made that perfectly clear, but what goes around comes around. One day she'll get what's due to her, you mark my words. I hope she burns in hell. They're all the same; Michelle and her group of cheating rats – one day they'll all get what's coming to them and I'll be the one pissing on them. I'll be the one laughing."

He is distraught. His face is red with anger and he swipes at the tears which are running down his cheeks. I don't know what to say. I just sit and stare at him.

"Sorry, I'm sorry," he eventually says and he holds up his hands in a placatory fashion. "This is not your problem."

Albert turns and walks away with his head held low and I wish he would disappear completely. His presence in town complicates things.

I'm so angry that Claude has been discussing me with Michelle, and as I sit waiting for him to arrive, I get increasingly angry. His indiscretion could cost me the whole deal. When he finally does arrive, I practically pounce on him.

He has barely sat down when I begin. "Why did you tell Michelle Moliner we were going into business together? I haven't yet given you my answer, and even if I do agree, it will be between us and nobody else. I'm really annoyed, Claude."

He looks at me sheepishly. "I didn't tell her any details," he says. "I just said we might do some business together. I didn't think you'd mind. Most people want to be involved with me professionally," he adds haughtily. His attitude enrages me even more.

"Most people? Like Doctor Poullet you mean?" I blurt. I'm shaking with rage. "Does he know you made money out of your little deal?"

Claude's face drains of all colour. "I'm not sure what you mean," he says, but the shocked expression on his face and his deathly pallor tells me he knows exactly what I mean.

"You remember the little deal, where Poullet euthanizes your clients and you reap the rewards?"

"Shh," he hisses and he looks around nervously to see if we've been overheard. "What has he said? How do you know? Has Falandry been in touch?"

"Poullet has told me everything, everything that is, except about you getting rich on the back of other people's misery of course. He doesn't know the finer details of that little arrangement, does he? I know exactly what you've been up to, because I have Gregory Armand's notes, and guess what Claude? You're named on every page. In answer to your third question, Falandry has been in touch, but I sent him packing."

"Thank God," Claude says. "If this ever got out, I'd be ruined and Poullet would go to jail. I knew you were reliable, that's why I chose you for the business deal. I know you'll be discreet and you won't let me down."

"Don't for one minute think I'm covering this up to help you," I reply. "The only reason I'm not arresting you right now is because of my good friend Poullet. He has been naïve and stupid, but he's done it for all the right reasons. You, on the other hand, are a greedy man with no compassion or conscience."

"So you don't want to help me with the business?" he states. "The terms I've offered are very fair and you'd have next to nothing to do. We could have made a load of money, but I understand if you want to walk away, given the circumstances."

"Don't be so quick, Claude," I reply. "You're not off the hook yet. Just sit there, say nothing and listen to what I have to say. When I finish telling you how things are going to be, you say, 'yes Danielle'. You will not argue and you will not try to negotiate. Do you understand?"

Claude is motionless, staring at me. He looks sick. "Yes, Danielle," he says.

"Firstly, you will tell Michelle Moliner that she made a mistake and we have no business dealings whatsoever. I don't want that woman knowing anything about my plans. Then you will find a way to discreetly search Albert's apartment to make sure there is nothing damning to be found there. Understand?"

He opens his mouth as if to speak, but I place my finger over his lips. "I said no talking," I warn.

Claude nods his head but stays silent.

"Good. Now about your offer. Patricia, my friend, will come to you with a proposition and you will accept it. First, I want you to tell me, with a yes or no answer – do you have access to ten thousand euros in cash?"

Claude looks confused but nods his agreement.

"Right," I say. "Patricia will offer you her services as project manager for the reconstruction. You will give her ten thousand euros in cash then she'll write you a cheque out of her business account for the same amount. This cheque will be shown on your books as her buying a share of the business, fifteen percent of the property and the same percentage of the profit. You will also write her a letter of engagement, which Boutiere will witness. Of course, you'll be selling her the share for a knock down price, but that's because you value her expertise and want to be sure she'll work with you. Patricia will project manage all the work, she'll do a good job and you'll pay her for her services. Do we have a deal?"

Claude does not move, but his right eye has developed a tic and his face is twitching.

"You may answer now," I say.

He swallows hard.

"Yes Danielle," I mouth the words, staring into his eyes and nodding slowly at him.

"Yes, Danielle," he replies.

I smile, lift a paper napkin from the table and offer it to Claude. He looks quizzically at it but takes it from me.

"Blackmail is a grubby business," I say. "And murder is much worse. But now you can wipe the blood off your hands."

Chapter 30

Over the next couple of days, all my plans come to fruition. Patricia's business is set up and her new bank account is opened with a transfer of ten thousand euros from her existing business account. The cash from Claude is stashed in our house, waiting to be trickled back into the bank over a period of weeks, so as not to give rise to money laundering questions – and Michelle Moliner is no longer my new best friend. I'm delighted that things have gone back to normal where she is concerned. We still exchange the same pleasantries when we meet, still greet each other with kisses to both cheeks, but that's as far as it goes. She no longer has time to sit and have coffee with me, or engage me in long conversations in the street. I don't know what Claude's said to her, but it's worked. It has taken him a while to get back to me about Albert, but eventually he telephones, to let me know he's searched his flat.

"The man is a pervert," Claude says, "He's depraved. The flat is full of pornographic magazines and films. And not just the usual top shelf stuff, sickening material that I'm sure must be banned."

"And does he have a penchant for boys or girls?" I ask, trying to seem cool when really I am embarrassed.

"Both," Claude says. "It's disgusting. I've also found photos of young women in various stages of undress. I think he's rigged up a camera in one of the changing rooms at the spa, because they look like they've been taken there. There was a whole shoe box full of them. I'm sure they've been snapped without the person knowing. I've removed the photographs and I'm going to check out the changing rooms to see if I can find a hidden camera. Albert will know I've been rummaging through his apartment, but I don't care. He can hardly complain given what I've found."

"And what about the information on your clients, did you find any notes or files?"

"No, nothing," he replies. "And I've destroyed any damaging information in the files and documents that I held."

"Good, then we've nothing to worry about because apart from Albert, only you, Poullet and I know the identity of the heart attack victims. We'll just have to hope that Albert disappears into obscurity when you evict him. We'll have to make sure he leaves town and doesn't come back. It's lucky he's a drunk because even if he tries to expose you, no one will believe him. Everyone will think he's just being bitter because he's lost his job."

"I hope you're right," Claude says. "I certainly don't want to lose everything at this stage. I've worked too hard for it."

"I think that's as far as we can go at the moment," I say. "We'll liaise again after the Christmas break. *Joyeux Noel et Bonne Annee*, Monsieur Claude."

"Yes," he replies. "And the same to you, Danielle."

I'm on call over the holidays, because I've decided to close the office from tomorrow, which is the twenty-third of December, until after Epiphany in January. Paul and Laurent are about to flip a coin to see who will deputise if I'm unavailable, but I don't really expect any of us to be called out. Marcel is making jokes and being incredibly annoying because being a trainee means he's off the hook. In the end, it is Paul who loses out.

"I think if anyone is called out over the holidays, Marcel should have to accompany them, as part of his training," Paul suggests.

135

"Yeah, yeah, very funny," Marcel replies. "Although it would probably save my sanity. I intend to be very drunk for several days, it's the only way I can cope with my family. At Christmas, all of a sudden, they become really boring and want to play stupid party games or watch rubbish on the television."

"You won't mind being on call then," I cut in. "I think you've made a splendid suggestion, Paul." Marcel's face freezes with a look of sheer horror. I'm only teasing, but his expression is hilarious. In a flash, Laurent has captured the image with his mobile phone.

"Let that be a lesson to you," Paul says laughing. "Be careful what you wish for."

"I'm not really on call, am I, Boss?" Marcel whines. "I was only joking about my family. My mother will kill me if I'm not at home for the holidays."

I try to keep a straight face as I stare at him and shrug.

"But, Boss," he moans. "My mother really will kill me."

The rest of us begin to laugh.

"You're joking, right? Very funny," Marcel says.

"Yes," I reply. "I am joking. You're not on call, but please try to be a bit more sensitive in future or when the next holiday comes around, you will be. It's easy to have fun at other people's expense, but it's not so amusing when the joke's on you. Oh, and by the way Laurent, I expect to see that very flattering photo you've just taken of Marcel posted on our community website," I add.

The jocularity continues for a while longer before we decide to call it a day. I send the boys home and lock up early. I've given Paul the day off tomorrow, to make up for him drawing the short straw over the holidays, so we exchange small gifts before he leaves.

I'll enjoy the next couple of days and I'll be able to relax because everything is organised and arranged. It will be nice to be able to put all thoughts of work out of my head and spend time with my friends and family. Even the prospect of my mother's company doesn't faze me, because I'm sure Byron will charm her and she'll be on her best behaviour. As I drive home, I feel rather smug and satisfied. This year looks like it's ending on a high.

Chapter 31

I automatically wake early on Christmas morning as if I were going to work before I remember I can enjoy the luxury of being able to roll over and go back to sleep. It's my first gift of the day. I easily sink back into oblivion because I am so relaxed and I haven't given in to the temptation of rising to check what the weather is like.

I wake again later with sunlight streaming through a crack in the curtains and the sound of Patricia moving about downstairs. I feel rather groggy – waking from a second sleep is often like that – but I know once I shower, I'll be fully awake and ready to enjoy the day.

Patricia and I only eat a light breakfast, because we're not very hungry. Last night we ate an enormous celebratory dinner before exchanging the main gifts that each of us had bought for the other. To my delight, I received a beautiful little writing desk, inlaid with marquetry. I'd seen the desk when I drove Byron to the *brocante* and I fell in love with it as soon as I clapped eyes on it, but I wouldn't part with its three-hundred-euro price tag to buy it for myself. My gift to Patricia was a very stylish garnet brooch to wear on her wool coat. She'd pointed it out to me when we were looking in the window of an antique shop in Ceret, and I returned and bought it later that day. Patricia was delighted with her gift, as she too, had returned to the shop intending to buy the brooch only to be disappointed when she'd found it was already sold. Today we plan to exchange the rest of our gifts when Byron and my parents arrive.

The house looks beautiful, Patricia has excelled herself. Decorated glass baubles hang from the window frames and an inviting log fire burns in the hearth. The table is laid out with a crisply-ironed, white linen tablecloth, topped with a rich gold table runner and gold place mats. She has made a decorative centrepiece using green foliage and red candles. Napkins of rich red linen and chair covers made from the same fabric finish off the scene. I compliment her work and Patricia smiles at me; she is very happy with her endeavours.

"Our guests are due to arrive at twelve-thirty to dine at one, but don't worry, everything's ready," she says.

"I didn't doubt that for one minute," I reply.

We wrap up warmly and take Ollee for a walk so he doesn't feel neglected later when he's restricted to the garden. It's extremely cold and there's even a flurry of snow.

"This is the first time I've ever seen a white Christmas," Patricia says. She links arms with me and her expression is one of soppy nostalgia. "It must be a good omen," she adds. "Jesus is smiling on us."

"Well, I don't know how that darned cat can see us from Sarah's house," I offer, making a joke. I don't want to mention anything religious when my mother is coming to visit. She could talk about sin for a month.

"You're terrible, Danielle," Patricia replies, slapping me on the arm. "You'd better watch out, or a lightning bolt might get you."

After we return to the house, we find ourselves pacing the floor with nervous anticipation. We want everything to be perfect, to prove to my parents that we are a family – Patricia, Ollee, Mimi and me. I particularly want my mother to see our home and homemaking skills. There is a fire in the hearth, the cat is lolling on the rug, the dog is chewing on a bone and Patricia and

139

I are beautifully attired. At twelve twenty-five we are leaning on the window ledge staring out of the window onto the street, eagerly anticipating the arrival of our guests. Curious about what is going on, Ollee pushes between us, and with paws on the ledge he jostles for position, so he too can see out.

"Have you remembered to chill the champagne?" Patricia asks.

"Yes," I reply. "And I've opened the red wine to let it breathe. Have you basted the turkey? We don't want it to dry out."

"The turkey's fine. Everything will be perfect. I'm just panicking."

"Me too," I say.

"Oh look, Danielle, that's Byron's car. He's just pulling up. Stand away from the window, we don't want them to know we've been looking out for them."

We take a step back, but we can still see them and we watch as Byron jumps out of the car to open the door for my mother, offering his arm for her to lean on. My parents are wearing their best clothes. Each is dressed in the outfits I bought for them when they attended an award ceremony to honour my work. Marjorie took them shopping for these clothes, and she has impeccable taste.

My father looks the same as always, his face is tanned from working outside in our orchard, but my mother looks frail. She isn't very old, but she seems to have developed the stoop of an elderly woman. Her face is lined and tired, and although her hair has been tinted, it looks thin and straggly. I'm sorry she's aging so quickly, but I can't help thinking that her mean spirit and venomous tongue have a lot to do with her deteriorating so quickly. My father always seems to disappoint her, and even though I'm very successful in my job and respected by the whole town, she can't find it in her heart to praise my achievements.

As we see them enter the gate, we open the front door to greet them. Ollee pushes past and runs up to my father, barking excitedly.

"Ollee, Ollee, my friend," Papa says, dropping to one knee and greeting the dog with pats to his head. "Did you miss me, boy? Did you miss me? Get your nose out of my pocket, there's nothing in there for you. Look at this cheeky dog. He thinks I've got food in my pocket."

"That's because you usually spoil him with treats," Patricia scolds. "Come in out of the cold. I'm so glad you're here," she adds.

It's clear from the moment she enters our home that my mother is on her best behaviour. There are no religious rants, no snide remarks about Patricia and me living together, and when she does say something, it's complimentary. By the time we're all seated and have been served our starter, I'm actually feeling relaxed and beginning to enjoy myself.

"You'll have to give me your recipe for this *sole filet terrine*, Patricia," mother says. "It's the best I've ever tasted. I used to prepare this for your Papa, Danielle, when I was a young woman. It's always been one of his favourites."

"The smoked salmon and the *foie gras* are good too," Byron adds. Then turning to my father, he adds, "This young lady is a superb cook, isn't she?"

"Yes," Papa replies, "The girls are wonderful homemakers and they're both so successful with their jobs and businesses. I don't know how they do it. Do you know my daughter mended the roof during that terrible storm? I wouldn't have had the courage to take on that task, but it was nothing to Danielle."

My mother's face pales. "You didn't go up on the roof during the storm, surely? You could have fallen, Danielle! You're just like your father, you know. He's always been a bit foolhardy. I think that's what made me fall in love with him in the first place. He was always the most daring of all the boys."

"And the most handsome," my father adds jokingly. Trying to cover his embarrassment at the compliment, but obviously delighted by what mother has said.

The main course is served amidst 'oohs' and 'aahs' of appreciation. The turkey is moist and cooked to perfection, the stuffing of pork, veal and chestnuts is mouth-watering and, by the time the *haricot vert*, peas, boiled chestnuts and diced, roast potatoes arrive, there isn't an inch of table not covered by some delicious offering.

"My my, dear girl, what a feast!" Byron compliments Patricia. "I've had the great pleasure of experiencing your culinary skills before, but this time you've excelled yourself. This is truly amazing."

Patricia is beaming. "Don't forget to leave room for cheese and then dessert," she says. "I know you have a sweet tooth," she adds, turning to Papa. "I've made your favourite pear flan, as well as the Yule log and we have some very good champagne to wash it down."

By four-thirty, we have moved from the table and are relaxing in armchairs by the fire with our coffees, liqueurs and truffles. The day could not have been better. Patricia is talking about her business deal with Monsieur Claude, and I'm delighted that my mother is taking an interest in what she's saying, because it means that by next week, the whole town will know.

"You've managed to negotiate a fantastic deal, Patricia," Byron says approvingly. "Claude must really need your input to sell you a fifteen per cent share at that price. Well done, young lady, very well done. You really are a force to be reckoned with in the business community."

"Danielle gives me confidence," Patricia replies graciously. "If it wasn't for her regular, good wage coming into the house, I wouldn't be able to take the chances that I do. We work as a team," she adds, winking at me.

"A formidable team," my Papa adds, smiling proudly.

The wind starts to whistle and it has grown very dark outside. Byron goes over to the window and peers out.

"It's snowing properly now," he says. "I'm sorry, but I think I should take your parents home, Danielle. I can't drive right up to their front door, as you know, with them living high up the hill in the old part of town. I think it will be for the best if we leave now. Your mother might struggle otherwise."

I agree with him, the weather is closing in. It's after six now anyway, and by the time Patricia and I clear up we'll be ready to sit and relax in our own company. I help my mother on with her coat, smoothing the fabric over her rail-thin shoulders.

"It's been a lovely day, Danielle. Thank you," she says.

I am thrilled, I'm ecstatic because my mother never pays me compliments. Papa leans over and kisses me on the forehead. "Well done, darling," he agrees. Byron plants smacking kisses on both of my cheeks then turns and does the same to Patricia. "Thank you for including me, dear girls," he says. "This has been a truly memorable day."

When I open the door a flurry of snow blows in on an icy blast of wind. Patricia and I grab our jackets and walk our guests to the car, watching as Byron drives off and the tail lights disappear down the hillside.

"We did it," Patricia says, sighing contentedly. "Even your mother enjoyed herself and not at the expense of the rest of us."

"Maybe Jesus is smiling on us, right enough," I reply.

"We'll have to phone Sarah and ask," she replies, quick as a flash.

Chapter 32

The snow lasted for three days, drawing adults and children alike out of their homes to play in it. It lay on the ground just long enough for us to enjoy the novelty, but when everyone rose on the fourth day to find it had rained through the night and the streets were washed clean, most people were delighted that things were back to normal.

I enjoyed such a peaceful yet joyous holiday, I almost forgot I'd have to return to the routine of work. When I opened the office for the first time in January, only my staff and I crossed the threshold the entire day. There were no phone calls, only a couple of automated emails and just advertising flyers in the post.

"We shouldn't have bothered coming in," Paul moans. "All we're doing is twiddling our thumbs."

"I couldn't agree more," I reply. "Why don't we take time off for at least another week? We can take turn about, two on and two off starting tomorrow. Just don't be seen getting drunk in the café when you should be working."

My suggestion is met with rousing cheers and it is quickly decided that Paul and Marcel will take the first break. When I arrive home after work, I'm surprised to find Monsieur Claude seated at the table, drinking coffee and eating apple pie.

"Monsieur Claude and I are just discussing our plans for the remodelling, Danielle," Patricia says. "It's a shame that Albert is living there, because apart from him, the building is empty. We can't begin the work until March because we can't evict him until then."

"Why don't you offer him some money to leave early? It shouldn't take much to get rid of him and I'm sure it would be worth your while."

"You're right, Danielle. That's a great idea. I simply hadn't thought of it. I'll phone him and suggest a meeting," Claude agrees.

Patricia beams at me and I can see she's really enjoying the discussion, but I wish she hadn't invited Claude here. I don't completely trust the man, especially now I know what he's been up to. Who knows what he's capable of?

When Claude leaves I offer Patricia a warning. "In the future, I'd rather you didn't meet Claude here. He shouldn't be seen coming to this house. I don't want anyone to think we're friends. I'd prefer it if you kept this business completely separate from our home life."

"I'm sorry Danielle," she says, "but I didn't invite him. He just turned up. In future if that happens I won't ask him in."

I'm annoyed at Claude and I intend to warn him off. How dare he arrive unannounced? I call Ollee for a walk, knowing Patricia is busy cooking.

"If you can wait half-an-hour I'll go with you," she says.

"Sorry," I reply, "but Ollee can't wait. We can go for another walk later if you'd like."

As soon as I'm clear of the house, I telephone Claude. When he answers, he chats away like a long-lost friend before he says, "What can I do for you, Danielle? Were you just phoning for a chat, or is there something you wish to discuss?"

I tread carefully, but let him know in no uncertain terms that any future meetings he has with Patricia must take place outside our home.

"Oh, I see," he replies. "I'm sorry, I didn't think, but of course no one can know we're involved. I'll think before I act next time."

"You and I are not involved, Claude. Let's be absolutely clear about that. We are acquaintances – nothing more. Agreed?"

"Yes, yes, of course. I've been presumptuous, it won't happen again."

"Good," I reply. "As long as we're clear."

I hang up the phone before he can say anything else. It's important that he knows who's in charge.

When I return from my walk, Marjorie has dropped in to give us our tickets for the journey to Glasgow and to show us the brochure of the hotel where we'll be staying. We're going to be in Scotland for three nights. Considering how quiet the office is, that should cause no problems at all.

"Doesn't the hotel look lovely?" Patricia says, smiling broadly. "It's in the city centre and the shops in Glasgow open every day, even on Sunday, even in winter. Marjorie says some supermarkets are open all day and all night! Imagine that!"

"It sounds marvellous," I agree, lifting my chequebook from my bag so I can pay Marjorie for the flights, but she won't hear of it.

"This trip is being paid for by Frances. He insists. He's very grateful to you girls for offering to attend Gilbert's wedding. Apart from us, no one from our side, either family or friends will be coming."

"But Marjorie!" I protest. "We're delighted to be invited. We're really looking forward to seeing them married. Please let me pay for our fares."

"Definitely not. Frances would be most upset if I let you. The hotel is booked and paid for too, courtesy of Gilbert and Stuart.

They're not short of money and they've paid for Stuart's close family's hotel rooms as well."

All I can do is thank Marjorie profusely. She waves her hand dismissively. "It's nothing," she says.

After Marjorie leaves, we spend the rest of the evening on the internet, researching our trip. We want to pack as much into our holiday as we can. Patricia has already purchased our wedding gift to the boys; matching pairs of silver cufflinks in a Celtic design. We know they'll be to their taste and they're easily carried in hand luggage. Fortunately, we both have suitable clothes to wear, so all I need do is tie up a few loose ends at work and we'll be ready to go and have fun.

Chapter 33

Three days after the end of the Christmas break – just when I think we'll never be busy again – I get a call from dispatch. I am given the address of Claude's apartment block and I'm asked to respond to an emergency call from the owner.

"The *pompiers* have already been summoned," the dispatcher says.

"Do we know what it's about?" I ask.

"Sorry, no," she replies. "The man was pretty incoherent. He just kept insisting that he needed the police and the *pompiers*. He said he'd already called for a doctor."

I lock up the office, and together with Marcel, we make our way to Claude's building.

"I wonder what's going on?" Marcel muses. "That Monsieur Claude is not very lucky. First the caretaker at his spa is murdered, then the detective investigating one of his clients is killed and now there's an incident requiring a doctor at another of his properties. Are you sure your friend should be going into business with this guy?"

We arrive at the building in minutes, because it's just around the corner from the office. I leave Marcel posted at the door and go inside to find Claude standing in the corridor outside a ground floor apartment. His face is ashen and he's holding a handkerchief to his mouth. It's evident from the splashes on his shoes that he's been sick.

"It's Albert, he's in there," he's says, nodding towards the open door. "Poullet's with him. He's dead. For some time, I think. I'm sorry, but I've been sick. The smell..." He is unable to complete the sentence and retches again.

I abandon Claude as he doubles up heaving and enter through the open door. Being a studio, it opens immediately into the main living room with the kitchen area to the left and a clic-clac sofa bed on the right. A large, walk-through double window leading to a balcony, is straight ahead. Poullet is standing beside the sofa bed staring at the decomposing body of Albert and holding his hand over his mouth and nose. Flies buzz around the corpse.

"I've opened the windows, but the smell is awful," he announces. "The body's been here for days, perhaps as long as a couple of weeks, judging by the infestation. The skin is bloated and slipping. I would suggest he killed himself. He's surrounded by empty booze and pill bottles. It's like a pharmacy in here, between sleeping pills and pain killers. Oh, and he left a note of sorts."

Poullet hands me a single sheet of writing paper. Written on it are the words, 'Dear Monsieur Claude, I'm sorry.'

"It's not much of a suicide note," I say. "He was a bit short on words, but I guess it implies his low mood."

"With the empty bottles of alcohol, the pill bottles and the note, I'm satisfied Albert killed himself. I'll get a report on what he's consumed, but I'm pretty sure it will prove he's ingested a fatal dosage."

I hear a siren draw near then stop; the *pompiers* have arrived. Within a minute, Jean is at my side.

"God, it stinks in here, it's nearly bad enough to put me off my lunch," he says. "What have we got, Doc?"

"Suicide, death by overdose of alcohol and drugs," Poullet replies.

"So the poor bugger died indulging in a party for one. I take it no one else was here. Who found him?"

"Monsieur Claude," I announce.

"He seems to have been the kiss of death recently," Jean replies.

"Please, let me pass," Poullet says. His face is a ghastly shade of green. "I have to get out of here. I'm not feeling too well." He staggers slightly as he exits the room and Jean's assistant grabs his arm to steady him. Poullet and Claude walk down the corridor towards the exit, leaving Jean and I alone.

"I hear you had lunch with one of my colleagues who is stationed further up the mountain," Jean says. "Jerome's a good man. Did you hear he's got back together with his partner? They'd separated, for nearly eight months I believe, but they're going to try again. They've got a little girl who's just started nursery school, so I hope it works out for them."

"Yes, me too," I reply. "I met him when Gregory Armand was killed. He does seem nice."

I'm trying to make small talk, but inside my heart is aching. Jerome didn't mention an ex-partner. I came very close to making a fool of myself and betraying Patricia over this man. I guess I've had a lucky escape, but I'm so disappointed.

I'm pleased when eventually I can leave the apartment and get back into the fresh air and for once, I'm relieved that Marcel is talking his usual rubbish on the way back to the office as it takes my mind off Jerome.

Chapter 34

We are now well into January and I've sent an email to Detective Gerard, to update him on my findings. I've told him I believe Bertrand Dupont was murdered and I suspect his killer to be Albert. It's well known that Albert hated Dupont and he certainly had the opportunity as he was probably the last person to leave the spa that day. We'll never know for sure, because Albert too, is now dead so we can't get the answers we need to confirm it. The autopsy proved that Albert swallowed a lethal overdose of drugs and alcohol and I suggest he probably took his own life because he was unable to live with the guilt.

In the case of Gregory Armand, I report that his death was simply the result of an unfortunate accident. Gerard is happy with my findings and he sends me an email saying I can now close these cases. He commends me on my good work and rightfully so. Once again I've handled everything successfully with little help.

My office is now functioning normally, with the holiday season well and truly over. Marcel has finished his training and he's been posted to an office north of Perpignan. I think he's an idiot, so I'm not unhappy to see the back of him.

During the Christmas break, Paul's cousin, Aileen, introduced him to one of her university friends. Marie-Louise, his new girlfriend, is a willowy blonde. She's very pretty and clever too, studying for a degree in psychology. Laurent and I tease Paul mercilessly, making jokes about Marie-Louise not actually wanting a boyfriend, but just needing someone crazy to study. Paul's so happy that nothing can burst his bubble and he hardly rises to the bait.

The work to convert the apartment building has been commissioned with a planned start date in February. Patricia is very excited, and as far as I can tell from speaking to Monsieur Claude, her ideas for the refit are stylish and inexpensive.

I've heard nothing from Jerome. He hasn't called me and maybe it's just as well. The chances of me running into him again are slim.

My mother and Papa have accepted a dinner invitation from Patricia. They will visit us when we return from Glasgow and this time I will collect them in my car. My mother now stops and speaks to me every time she sees me in the street instead of crossing the road or hurrying past with a wave of her hand. I find her friendliness unnerving but I'm sure I'll get used to it in the fullness of time. We will never be close. There's been too much water under the bridge for that.

Patricia and I are sitting at the dining table with all our leaflets and notes about Glasgow spread out in front of us. We are excitedly looking forward to our trip which begins in two day's time. I'm devouring my second piece of almond tart and we've almost finished drinking one of Freddy's excellent bottles of wine when Patricia speaks. "It's a shame Bertrand Dupont died at the spa. Claude is having a hard time getting over it. And now, with Albert killing himself, he has to find a caretaker soon or he won't be able to re-open in February."

"I'm sure people will be queuing up for the job," I reply. "There are lots of folk out of work and it doesn't take too much skill to mop a floor or clean a pool."

"I suppose your right," she says. "Oh, and someone called Falandry keeps phoning Claude. I'm not exactly sure what it's about, but I think it's something to do with Falandry's ex-wife. Wasn't that man Gregory Armand asking about her? You remember, the man who accidentally crashed his car over the side of the mountain."

I look at Patricia's sweet face. I think it's time I told her what happened at the spa. I feel she should know. It's not fair to keep her in the dark any longer.

"I have something to tell you, Patricia," I say. "I love you and trust you and you know you're the most important person in the world to me."

"Is it about Jerome?" she asks and I see a flash of fear cross her face. "Have you been seeing him? You haven't mentioned his name for a while."

"No, no, darling, nothing like that. I haven't mentioned him because I have only had one lunch with the man. He has a partner and a daughter. What made you think I was seeing him?"

"Nothing, really, I was just worried. I thought you were attracted to him, that's all."

"Darling, I love formula one racing cars, but I wouldn't want to drive one and I can admire someone without wanting to date them."

Her face visibly relaxes. "I'm sorry," she says. "I've been such a fool. I'm so sorry. What was it you wanted to tell me?"

"I want to tell you the truth about Doctor Poullet and Monsieur Claude," I begin. "There's no easy way to say this, but together they've committed a crime and I've covered it up to save them from going to jail. I've taken a chance, because I'm confident the truth will never get out."

"What did they do that would be serious enough for them to go to jail? I can't imagine either of them committing a crime," she replies.

"Oh darling, if only that were true," I say. "I'm afraid this will shock you. I couldn't believe it myself, but Doctor Poullet has killed four people and Claude has aided and abetted him."

"What? Did you say Poullet has killed people? How? Why?"

"He treated four very sick people, they were terminally ill, actually. He took away their pain and suffering by ending their lives. It was done with compassion and he didn't receive any payment. Poullet euthanized four souls who had no hope left and who were losing their dignity and Claude allowed it to take place at the spa."

"So, the people wanted to die?"

"Absolutely. They approached Poullet and begged for his help to end their suffering."

"And you found out and covered it up?"

"Yes."

"What has Monsieur Falandry got to do with all this?" she asks.

I explain about Gregory Armand and the notes I kept from his car.

"So, if Armand had lived, this whole sordid mess would have been exposed?" she questions. "But because he was killed and you kept the notes, nobody will ever discover the truth."

"Exactly," I reply. "I've been carrying the secret about with me for weeks. But I had to tell you the truth, because Poullet is your physician and Claude is your new business partner. Can you forgive me for not sharing it with you sooner?"

Patricia takes my hands in hers and kisses them. "My poor darling," she says. "What a terrible thing to happen. Poullet is your friend and now you know he has taken lives. How brave and loyal of you to protect him. He's a kind man and I can understand him helping others, but Claude surprises me. I didn't think he would assist anyone, unless he was making money out of it. Look how he treated Albert."

I'm so relieved she's not upset with me; quite the contrary, she's sorry I had to carry such a burden alone.

"I have to agree with you about Claude," I reply. "But it's all over now. The cases are closed. Poullet will not assist anyone else to die and Claude is going to make you a lot of money. There's only Falandry left to ask questions and he will soon tire of his quest, when he consistently reaches dead ends."

We open another bottle of wine and return to discussing our holiday. I feel unburdened and free once again. Patricia is happy, I am happy and the world is turning just as it should.

Chapter 35

ANOTHER TRUTH

If I hadn't been standing outside the spa at the end of that particular working day, I wouldn't have known Albert was innocent of Dupont's death. I saw him leave the building, you see, and as he stepped outside, I heard him call out *au revoir*', just as Monsieur Claude described in his statement. Within a minute or two of him closing the door and walking away, I saw Dupont arrive and enter the building. It was strange to see him dressed in his suit. I didn't know it then, but I know now that Dupont had gone home to change before his meeting with Claude, perhaps to add gravitas to their conversation. I can only assume that Dupont tried to blackmail Claude. I know he was probably questioning how unlikely it was that all these people to die from fatal heart attacks within such a short space of time. If Dupont was capable of beating his wife, blackmail would have been easy for him. I'll never know why they were at the pool area, and not in the office. Was it always Claude's intention to lead Dupont to his death? Perhaps he'd admitted the truth to him before he bashed in his head and then drowned him, but maybe not. Maybe it was a knee jerk reaction with no time for chit-chat. Whatever the case, one thing I'm sure of is that Monsieur Claude killed Bertrand Dupont. I've kept this piece of information to myself, tucking it away for safekeeping. Who knows when I'll want to bring it back out for an airing?

The day I went looking for Poullet, but instead met Claude coming out of the car park wiping his hands on a rag, I didn't immediately know what he was up to – but when Armand was killed, I put two and two together. I recognised the smell, you see. It was brake fluid on the rag, not oil. I'm not sure if Claude actually intended to kill Armand, or merely scare him, but in either case, his actions solved one problem – permanently.

From the minute I found out about Madame Falandry's house and the various lumps of money Claude had been left, I knew I was onto a winner. I wasn't certain at that stage how I was going to benefit from it, but I knew that in the fullness of time, I'd work it out.

The only spoke left in the wheel – the only person remaining who could cause me problems, – was Albert. He was not a good man. He was depraved and creepy and I knew he could turn out to be extremely dangerous. I hated his drunkenness, it made him unpredictable, and I couldn't risk having a loose canon shooting his mouth off. It seemed only fitting that he would meet his end by drinking himself into oblivion. True, I helped him on his way. I don't know how many tablets I crushed into the bottles of brandy I gave him at Christmas, but it was easily enough to kill a horse. I knew he'd drink the lot. He was delighted to see me and pathetically grateful when I visited his apartment. I suggested he write to Claude, apologising for his actions and asking for his job back. I lied and told him I'd add my support. As soon as he'd written the first few words, I took the paper from him and handed him one of the bottles. He gulped down the golden liquid, emptying half the contents in a matter of seconds. It didn't even touch the sides. As I left his apartment, I lifted his key so I could return later to set the scene. It needed to look like suicide. I didn't want to hang around, but I had to be able to re-enter his home and make sure he'd done the job properly. I had to be sure he was dead.

I couldn't believe how long it took for his body to be discovered. I was beginning to think he'd never be found.

Still, patience is a virtue and everything comes to he, or she, who waits.

A Message from Danielle

Thank you for reading 'Dead End in the Pyrenees,' I do hope you enjoyed it. If you've read the first three books in the 'Death in the Pyrenees' series you will know the journey I've travelled to reach this stage and what a journey it has been. However, if you've had no previous knowledge of my life and would like to catch up with my ups and downs and highs and lows, you can meet my friends and colleagues and some of the less desirable individuals who have lived and died here - available now other books of the series and Elly Grant's other novels.

Till soon
Danielle

Other books by Elly Grant

Palm Trees in the Pyrenees
Take one rookie female cop
Add a dash or two of mysterious death
And a heap of prejudice and suspicion
Place all in a small French spa town
And stir well
Turn up the heat
And simmer until thoroughly cooked
The result will be surprising

Grass Grows in the Pyrenees gives an insight into the workings and atmosphere of a small French town and the surrounding mountains, in the Eastern Pyrenees. The story unfolds told by Danielle, a single, thirty-year-old, cop. The sudden and mysterious death of a local farmer suspected of growing cannabis opens a 'Pandora's' box of trouble. It's a race against time to stop the gangsters before the town, and everyone in it, is damaged beyond repair.

sample - Chapter 1

His death occurred quickly and almost silently. It took only seconds of tumbling and clawing at air before the inevitable thud as he hit the ground. He landed in the space in front of the bedroom window of the basement apartment. As no-one was home at the time and, as the flat was actually below ground level, he may have gone unnoticed but for the insistent yapping of the scrawny, aged poodle belonging to the equally scrawny and aged Madame Laurent.

Indeed, everything in the town continued as normal for a few moments. The husbands who'd been sent to collect the baguettes for breakfast had stopped, as usual, at the bar to enjoy a customary glass of pastis and a chat with the patron and other customers. Women gathered in the little square beside the river, where the daily produce market took place, to haggle for fruit, vegetables and honey before moving the queue to the boucherie to choose the meat for their evening meals.

Yes, that day began like any other. It was a cold, crisp, February morning and the sky was a bright, clear blue just as it had been every morning since the start of the year. The yellow Mimosa shone out luminously in the morning sunshine from the dark green of the Pyrenees.

Gradually, word filtered out of the boucherie and down the line of waiting women that the first spring lamb of the season had made its way onto the butcher's counter and everyone wanted some. Conversation switched from whether Madame Portes actually grew the Brussels sprouts she sold on her stall, or simply bought them at the supermarket in Perpignan then resold them at a higher price, to speculating whether or not there would be sufficient lamb to go round. A notable panic rippled down the queue at the very thought of there not being enough as none of the women wanted to disappoint her family. That would be unacceptable in this small Pyrenean spa town, as in this small town, like many others in the region a woman's place as housewife and mother was esteemed and revered. Even though many held jobs outside the home, their responsibility to their family was paramount.

Yes, everyone followed their usual routine until the siren blared out – twice. The siren was a wartime relic that had never been decommissioned even though the war had ended over half a century before. It was retained as a means of summoning the pompiers, who were not only the local firemen but also paramedics. One blast of the siren was used when there was a minor road accident or if someone took unwell at the spa but two blasts was for something extremely serious.

The last time there were two blasts was when a very drunken Jean-Claude accidentally shot Monsieur Reynard while mistaking him for a boar. Fortunately Monsieur Reynard recovered, but he still had a piece of shot lodged in his head which caused his eye to squint when he was tired. This served as a constant reminder to Jean-Claude of what he'd done as he had to see Monsieur Reynard every day in the cherry orchard where they both worked.

On hearing two blasts of the siren everyone stopped in their tracks and everything seemed to stand still. A hush fell over the town as people strained to listen for the shrill sounds of the approaching emergency vehicles. Some craned their necks skyward hoping to see the police helicopter arrive from Perpignan and, whilst all were shocked that something serious had occurred, they were also thrilled by the prospect of exciting, breaking news. Gradually, the chattering restarted. Shopping was forgotten and the market abandoned. The boucherie was left unattended as its patron followed the crowd of women making their way to the main street. In the bar the glasses of pastis were hastily swallowed instead of being leisurely sipped as everyone rushed to see what had happened.

As well as police and pompiers, a large and rather confused group of onlookers arrived outside an apartment building owned by an English couple called Carter. They arrived on foot and on bicycles. They brought ageing relatives, pre-school children, prams and shopping. Some even brought their dogs. Everyone peered and stared and chatted to each other. It was like a party without the balloons or streamers.

There was a buzz of nervous excitement as the police from the neighbouring larger town began to cordon off the area around the apartment block with tape. Monsieur Brune was told in no uncertain terms to restrain his dog, as it kept running over to where the body lay, and was contaminating the area in more ways than one.

A slim woman wearing a crumpled linen dress was sitting on a chair in the paved garden of the apartment block, just inside the police line. Her elbows rested on her knees and she held her head in her hands. Her limp, brown hair hung over her face. Every so often she lifted her chin, opened her eyes and took in great, gasping breaths of air as if she was in danger of suffocating. Her whole body shook. Madame Carter, Belinda, hadn't actually fainted but she was close to it. Her skin was clammy and her pallor grey. Her eyes threatened at any moment to roll back in their sockets and blot out the horror of what she'd just seen.

She was being supported by her husband, David, who was visibly shocked. His tall frame sagged as if his thin legs could no longer support his weight and he kept swiping away tears from his face with the backs of his hands. He looked dazed and, from time to time, he covered his mouth with his hand as if trying to hold in his emotions but he was completely overcome.

The noise from the crowd became louder and more excitable and words like accident, suicide and even murder abounded. Claudette, the owner of the bar that stood across the street from the incident, supplied the chair on which Belinda now sat. She realized that she was in a very privileged position, being inside the police line, so Claudette stayed close to the chair and Belinda. She patted the back of Belinda's hand distractedly, while endeavouring to overhear tasty morsels of conversation to pass on to her rapt audience. The day was turning into a circus and everyone wanted to be part of the show.

Finally, a specialist team arrived. There were detectives, uniformed officers, secretaries, people who dealt with forensics and even a dog handler. The tiny police office was not big enough to hold them all so they commandeered a room at the Mairie, which is our town hall.

It took the detectives three days to take statements and talk to the people who were present in the building when the man, named Steven Gold, fell. Three days of eating in local restaurants and drinking in the bars much to the delight of the proprietors. I presumed these privileged few had expense accounts, a facility we local police did not enjoy. I assumed that my hard earned taxes paid for these expense accounts yet none of my so called colleagues asked me to join them.

They were constantly being accosted by members of the public and pumped for information. Indeed everyone in the town wanted to be their friend and be a party to a secret they could pass on to someone else. There was a buzz of excitement about the place that I hadn't experienced for a very long time. People who hadn't attended church for years suddenly wanted to speak to the priest. The doctor who'd attended the corpse had a full appointment book. And everyone wanted to buy me a drink so they could ask me questions. I thought it would never end. But it did. As quickly as it had started, everybody packed up, and then they were gone.

Grass Grows in the Pyrenees
Take one female cop and
Add a dash of power
Throw in a dangerous gangster
Some violent men
And a whole bunch of cannabis
Sprinkle around a small French spa town
And mix thoroughly
Cook on a hot grill until the truth is revealed

Grass Grows in the Pyrenees gives an insight into the workings and atmosphere of a small French town and the surrounding mountains, in the Eastern Pyrenees. The story unfolds told by Danielle, a single, thirty-year-old, cop. The sudden and mysterious death of a local farmer suspected of growing cannabis opens a 'Pandora's' box of trouble. It's a race against time to stop the gangsters before the town, and everyone in it, is damaged beyond repair.

sample - Chapter 1

For a moment, he flew horizontally as if launched like a paper aeroplane from the mountain top then an elegant swan dive carried him over the craggy stone face of the mountainside. There was no thrashing of limbs or clawing at air; he fell silently and gracefully until a sickening crack echoed through the valley as bone and flesh crunched and crumpled on a rocky outcrop. The impact bounced him into the air and flipped him in a perfect somersault, knocking the shoes from his feet. Then he continued his descent until he came into contact with the grassy slope near the bottom of the mountain, where he skidded and rolled before coming to a halt against a rock.

His body lay on its back in an untidy heap with arms and legs and shoulders and hips smashed and broken. The bones stuck out at impossible angles and blood pooled around him. He lay like that for almost three days. During that time the vultures had a feast. There are several species of these birds in the mountains of the Pyrenees and all had their fill of him. Rodents and insects had also taken their toll on the body and, by the time he was discovered, he was unrecognisable.

A hunter found him while walking with his dog and, although he was used to seeing death, the sight of this man's ravaged face, with black holes where his eyes should have been, made him vomit.

Jean-Luc still wore the suit that he'd carefully dressed in for his meeting three days before. It looked incongruous on him in his present condition and in these surroundings. His wallet was still in his pocket and his wedding ring was still on his finger; nothing had been stolen.

The alarm had been raised by his business partner when he failed to turn up for their meeting but of course no one had searched for him in this place. This valley was outside of town and on the other side of the mountain from where he'd lived. He wasn't meant to be anywhere near to this place.

His wife hadn't been overly concerned when he didn't return because he often went on drinking binges with his cronies and he'd disappeared for several days on other occasions. She was just pleased if he eventually came home sober because he had a foul temper and he was a very nasty drunk. Indeed, she knew how to make herself scarce when he was drunk, as more often than not, she would feel the impact of a well-aimed punch or a kick. Drunk or sober, he lashed out with deadly accuracy and he was quick on his feet.

When he was finally discovered, all the emergency services were called into action. The pompiers, who were firemen and trained paramedics, the police and the doctor all arrived at the scene and an ambulance was summoned to remove the body to the morgue.

Everyone assumed he'd died as a result of his rapid descent from the mountain top and the subsequent impact on the ground below. But what they all wanted to know was whether his death was a tragic accident, or suicide, or perhaps something darker and more sinister, and why was he in this place so far from his home or from town? Many questions had to be answered and being the most senior police officer in this area meant that I was the person who'd be asking the questions.

Red Light in the Pyrenees
Take one respected female cop
Add two or three drops of violent death
Some ladies of the night

And a bucket full of blood
Place all in, and around, a small French spa town
Stir constantly with money and greed
Until all becomes clear
The result will be very satisfying

Red light in the Pyrenees, third in the series Death in the Pyrenees, gives you an insight into the workings and atmosphere of a small French town in the Eastern Pyrenees. The story unfolds, told by Danielle, a single, thirty-something, female cop. The sudden and violent death of a local Madam brings fear to her working girls and unsettles the town. But doesn't every cloud have a silver lining? Danielle follows the twists and turns of events until a surprising truth is revealed. Hold your breath, it's a bumpy ride.

sample – Chapter 1

The body of Madame Henriette is lying through the broken window of the kitchen door with the lower part of the frame supporting her lifeless corpse. Her head, shoulder and one arm hang outside, while the rest of her remains inside, as if she has endeavoured to fly, Superman style, through the window and become stuck. She is slumped, slightly bent at the knees, but with both feet still touching the floor. Her body is surrounded by jagged shards of broken glass.

From the kitchen this is all one sees. It is not until you open the window to the side of the door and look through it, that you see the blood. Indeed quite a large area of the tiny courtyard has been spattered with gore as Madame Henriette's life has pumped out of her. One shard has sliced through her throat and by the amount of blood around, it seems to have severed her jugular. She must have been rendered unconscious almost immediately as she has made no effort to lift herself off the dagger-like pieces of glass which are sticking out from the frame.

There is blood on the pot plants and on the flowering creeper which grows up the wall, dividing this house from the neighbour's. It has also sprayed the small, hand crafted, wrought iron table and chairs. The blood is beginning to turn black in the morning sun and there's a sizeable puddle congealing on the ground under the body. This will need to be spread with sawdust when the clean up begins, I think to myself.

There is rather a lot of blood on Madame Henriette's head as it has run down her face from the gaping wound on her throat, but it's still possible to see that her hair is well-styled and her face is fully made up. Her clothes are tight and rather too sexy for a woman of her age and her push-up bra and fish-net stockings seem inappropriate at this time of the morning. If you didn't know any better, you would assume that Madame Henriette is simply a lady of growing years trying desperately to hold on to her youth, but to her neighbours and those of us who have had dealings with her, the truth is much less forgiving. Madame Henriette is indeed a Madame. She is a lady of the night, a peddler of prostitutes, and this building which she owns is a brothel.

The house of Madame Henriette is situated in the old part of town where the cobbled streets are so narrow that only one car may pass at a time. All the buildings are tall and slim and made of stone. Each is distinguished from the next by different coloured shutters and different degrees of weathering to the facade.

When entering this house one would pass through a small door which is cut in a much larger, heavier one. The magnificent carved entrance looks overdressed in this street and harks back to a time when this area was much grander. Nowadays everyone wants modern and the town has spread out with alarming speed from this central point. The wealthy live in the suburbs. They have gardens, swimming pools and pizza ovens. From once being uptown and chic, these streets have become dreary and they now contain a lower class of citizen. They are a melting pot of students, foreigners and people who survive on state benefits.

Sometimes holidaymakers rent here thinking the area is quaint and having the desire to experience a 'typical' French house in a 'typical' French street.

After entering through the door, which is immediately off the road, you would find yourself in a narrow hallway with a magnificent, old and ornate, tiled floor. A curved stone stairway with an iron banister rail then takes you to the upper floors. On the first floor, if you turned to your right, you would find yourself in the sitting room where Madame Henriette offered her guests some wine as they waited for one of her 'nieces' to fetch them. Then they would be taken to one of the bedrooms which are situated on the upper floors. To the left is the kitchen but few meals were cooked there. Food was usually very quickly thrown together from a selection of cold meats, cheese and bread, then hastily eaten by the girls as they grabbed a few spare moments between clients. All, of course, was washed down with glasses of heavy, red, cheap, local wine. The wine made both the food and the clients more palatable.

The body of Madame Henriette was discovered by her maid Eva who is a rather scrawny girl aged about twenty. She has mousy brown hair and grubby looking skin peppered with acne scars. Every day Eva came to work for Madame, her duties being to wash the sheets, clean the house and bring in the food from the market. She was also responsible for buying condoms and checking that each bedroom had a plentiful supply. Madame Henriette was fastidious about health and safety and would never allow sexual contact without condoms.

On discovering the body of her mistress, the shocked young woman fled the house and ran screaming into the street. One of the neighbours heard the screams and chose, on this occasion, not to ignore the noises coming from the vicinity of the house but instead telephoned for the emergency services and this is where my story begins.

Deadly Degrees in the Pyrenees

The ghastly murder of a local estate agent reveals unscrupulous business deals which have the whole town talking. Michelle Moliner was not liked, but why would someone want to kill her? The story unfolds, told by Danielle, a single, thirty-something, female cop based in a small French town in the Eastern Pyrenees. Danielle's friends may be in danger and she must discover who the killer is before anyone else is harmed.

Deadly Degrees in the Pyrenees is the 5th book in the Death in the Pyrenees series. It's about life, local events, colourful characters, prejudice and of course death in a small French town

sample – Chapter 1

When the woman first began to feel too hot she tried to tough it out convincing herself she could take it and besides the sauna was great for her skin, but after another few minutes she knew she'd had enough. Her face was flushed, her temperature raised and sweat was no longer forming in droplets on her skin. Definitely time to call it a day, she thought.

Pushing on the door she was surprised to find it unyielding. Sauna doors are designed to withstand extreme changes in temperature. They do not warp. The woman put her shoulder to it. Still it didn't budge. Her stomach began to cramp and fear crept in. Why was the door stuck? How could it be stuck? She stared out of the tempered, safety-glass panel.

"Help, help," she called banging on the glass. "Is anybody there? Help, help me, I'm stuck in the sauna." She paused, listening, but she heard no sounds, there was only silence.

Realising her plight she began to panic and scream, long keening animal-like sounds. Her temperature rose even higher. Painful spasms wracked her legs and hands. She became confused, throwing herself against the side walls of the sauna in an attempt to escape then trying to kick her way out by pounding her bare heels on the wooden floor.

Eventually, she collapsed with exhaustion and heat stroke. She lost consciousness and fell into a coma before her body succumbed to shock.

Her corpse was discovered hours later when her lover arrived for a romantic liaison. There was nothing romantic about what he found. The ghastly sight of the broiled woman with her red skin and bulging bloodshot eyes would stay with him for the rest of his life.

Michelle Moliner's murderer had planned to kill her. This was not an accident, not a random act of burglary gone wrong. Her killer knew she'd be alone and vulnerable. Her killer wanted her to burn in Hell.

* * *

It had been a beautiful morning. The sun was shining through a chink in the curtains. Michelle stretched lazily, spreading out her limbs in the comfortable king-sized bed. Even though she and Jacques no longer shared a bedroom she was pleased he had gone away with his club and she had the house to herself. Michelle planned to have a gloriously indulgent day. She had first stirred when Jacques banged about the house getting ready for his weekend. He was a clumsy man and didn't make any effort to be quiet on her account. She heard the front door slam, the squeal from the hinges of the tall, electrically controlled, double gates that enclosed the driveway then his car revving before driving off. Michelle knew that the front door would not be locked as Jacques would have merely pulled it closed as he left, but she was surprised that there was no clunk from the gates closing. It amazed her that he'd installed the gates to stop any of his precious cars being driven away and stolen, yet the house with all her precious contents was left unprotected. It was clear where his priorities lay. Now she was fully awake having been able to grab an extra hour of blissful slumber once all had eventually become quiet once again.

Michelle had planned the perfect day. She'd made a list in her head of her regime for the next few hours making full use of the trappings of wealth she enjoyed. There was her beautiful swimming pool, the hot-tub, the sauna and enough creams and lotions to satisfy the whole town. Everyone knew that her home was sensational because Michelle constantly reminded them. She wasn't liked, many hated her, but all were rather frightened of her and that's the way she liked it.

Michelle Moliner enjoyed being rich. She loved the power of wealth. Apart from the mayor's wife, who she considered to be her equal, Michelle thought she was probably the most important woman in the area. But she didn't always hold the position she now enjoyed. As a child, being the fourth daughter of a local cheese merchant, she was way down the pecking order. But Michelle was smart, smart enough to realise the value of marrying well. Jacques Moliner was not as clever as Michelle, but he was an only son and his father was blessed with amazing luck and the ability to turn muck into brass. Jacques' father amassed a huge fortune then conveniently died young, leaving everything divided equally between his wife and his son. Within one month of her husband's demise Madame Moliner had a massive heart attack and was promptly buried beside him. Jacques didn't grieve for long however, his bulging bank account soon helped to dry his tears.

He'd always liked Michelle although on and off he'd dated her sister, Helene. In fact everyone expected him to one day marry Helene. Michelle was petite and pretty and, being rather shy, Jacques appreciated the cute young woman who found him so fascinating. She persuaded him to end things once and for all with Helene then tempted him with the promise of dirty sex, but only after they were married of course. Helene was not pleased but there was nothing she could do. Michelle hooked Jacques as easily as if he'd jumped on the line and played dead.

Everyone suspected that Michelle found the money more attractive than the man. They all said, those wagging-tongued, jealous bitches, that it wouldn't last and many prayed for the opportunity of stepping into Michelle's shoes. And they were partly right. The sex didn't last and neither did the promise of love ever after, but they underestimated Michelle's tenacity. There was no way she would leave Jacques, not while one single centime remained in the bank account they shared. So the couple continued to live together, yet apart, in the fabulous house they jointly owned and, while Jacques frequently travelled away with the vintage car club, Michelle entertained her current lover and spent more and more of their joint cash, while all of her own earnings were being saved in a secret account in Spain.

But none of that mattered any more. Michelle was beyond caring. One callous act, one murderous act had ended her life and everything she'd worked for.

* * *

When I received the call from the dispatcher I responded immediately. Accompanied by my assistant Laurent, I left the office and we drove to Michelle Moliner's house. Laurent was excited to be going with me. He, like many others, had speculated about Madame Moliner's home. Only a privileged few, her inner circle, her employees and her husband's close friends, had ever been invited to enter through the large iron security gates and be welcomed at the 'castel'.

But, forgive me please, I am rambling on before we have been formally introduced. Allow me to rectify that. My name is Danielle and I am the senior police officer in charge of this region. I oversee my small town which is situated on the French side of the Eastern Pyrenees. I also look after several villages and farms, quite a large area, in fact. I'm smart and in my thirties, still quite young, but it's been a struggle to reach the esteemed position I now enjoy. Women do not usually reach the higher echelons here and in particular, women who are young and unmarried.

I live with my friend Patricia in a lovely home on the edge of town. It is close enough for me to walk to work but far enough away from the gossipers and the prying eyes. Not that I have anything to hide, our friendship is that of sisters even though Patricia is a lesbian, but you know how people like to talk.

Anyway, I am rambling again. Apart from Guy Legler who was Michelle's lover, Laurent and I were the first to arrive at the scene. We found Monsieur Legler in a state of deep shock and no wonder, the sight that greeted us was ghastly. I have never seen a person cooked before and I hope I never have to witness such a thing again. Within a few minutes the medical emergency team arrived, closely followed by the 'pompiers' who are firemen and trained paramedics. There is nothing anyone can do. Michelle has been dead for several hours.

I arrange for Monsieur Legler to be taken to the clinic for treatment and send the medical emergency team away. I tell Laurent to return to the office. He is not happy about being dismissed as he'd like time to look around this house, but too bad, I am the boss and he must do as he is told. Besides he is a bungler, a bit of a buffoon and he irritates me.

I wait at the house with my old friend Jean, who is in charge of the pompiers. We have attended many scenes of death before and, apart from the unfortunate circumstances of our meetings, we enjoy spending the time together, passing a few hours chatting. We must wait now for a medical examiner to attend the corpse before we can move on. My old friend Doctor Poullet has been summoned, but we have no idea when he will arrive.

Jean and I sit in the landscaped garden in the sunshine and we discuss the petanque club's forthcoming barbecue and the cycle race which is being held next month and the poor condition of the main road through town and indeed, anything else that springs to mind as we await the good doctor's arrival.

The Unravelling of Thomas Malone

The mutilated corpse of a young prostitute is discovered in a squalid apartment.

Angela Murphy has recently started working as a detective on the mean streets of Glasgow. Just days into the job she's called to attend this grisly murder. She is shocked by the horror of the scene. It's a ghastly sight of blood and despair.

To her boss, Frank Martin, there's something horribly familiar about the scene.

Is this the work of a copycat killer?

Will he strike again?

With limited resources and practically no experience, Angela is desperate to prove herself.

But is her enthusiasm sufficient?

Can she succeed before the killer strikes again?

and here's the first few pages to sample -

Prologue

Thomas Malone remembered very clearly the first time he heard the voice. He was twelve years, five months and three days old. He knew that for a fact because it was January 15th, the same day his mother died.

Thomas lived with his mother Clare in the south side of Glasgow. Their home was a main door apartment in a Victorian terrace. The area had never been grand, but in its time, it housed many incomers to the city. First the Irish, then Jews escaping from Eastern Europe, Italians, Polish, Greeks, Pakistanis, they'd all lived there and built communities. Many of these families became the backbone of Glasgow society. However situations changed and governments came and went and now the same terraces were the dumping ground for economic migrants who had no intention of working legally, but sought an easy existence within the soft welfare state system.

A large number of the properties were in the hands of unscrupulous landlords who were only interested in making money. They didn't care who they housed as long as the rent was paid. So as well as the people fleeing the system, there were also the vulnerable who they exploited. Drug addicts, alcoholics, prostitutes, young single mothers with no support, they were easy pickings for the gangsters. The whole area and the people living within it smacked of decay. It had become a no-go district for decent folk, but to Thomas Malone, it was simply home.

Thomas and his mother moved to their apartment on Westmoreland Street when Clare fell out with her parents. The truth was they really didn't want their wayward daughter living with them any more. They were embarrassed by her friends and hated their drinking and loud music. When Clare became pregnant, it was the last straw. Thomas's grandparents were honest, hard-working, middle-class people who had two other children living at home to consider. So when Clare stormed out one day after yet another row with her mother, they let her go. She waited in a hostel for homeless women for three weeks before she realised they weren't coming to fetch her home and that's when Clare finally grew up and took charge of her life in the only way she knew how.

When Thomas walked home from school along Westmoreland Street, he didn't see that the building's façades were weather worn and blackened with grime from traffic fumes. To outsiders they looked shabby and were reminiscent of a mouth full of rotting teeth, but to Thomas they were familiar and comforting. He didn't notice the litter strewn on the road, the odd discarded shoe, rags snagged on railings, or graffiti declaring 'Joe's a wanker' or 'Mags a slag'. He functioned, each day like the one before, never asking for anything because there was never any money to spare.

He was used to the many 'uncles' who visited his mother. Some were kind to him and gave him money to go to the cinema, but many were drunken and violent. Thomas knew to keep away from them. Sometimes he slept on the stairs in the close rather than in his bed so he could avoid any conflict. He kept a blanket and a cushion in a cardboard box by the door for such occasions. Many a time, when he returned from school, he found his mother with her face battered and bruised crying because the latest 'uncle' had left, never to return. It was far from being an ideal life, but it was all he knew so he had no other expectations.

It was a very cold day and, as he hurried home from school, Thomas's breath froze in great puffs in front of him. He was a skinny boy, small for his age with pixie features common to children of alcoholics. His school shirt and thin blazer did little to keep him warm and he rubbed his bare hands together in an attempt to stop them from hurting. He was glad his school bag was a rucksack because he could sling it over his shoulder to protect his back from the icy wind. As his home drew near his fast walk became a jog, then a run, his lungs were sore from inhaling the cold air, but he didn't care, he would soon be indoors. He would soon be able to open and heat a tin of soup for his dinner and it would fill him up and warm him through. He hoped his mother had remembered to buy some bread to dunk.

As Thomas approached the front door something didn't seem right, he could see that it was slightly ajar and the door was usually kept locked. There was a shoe shaped imprint on the front step, it was red and sticky and Thomas thought it might be blood. There was a red smear on the cream paint of the door frame, he was sure it was blood. Thomas pushed the door and it opened with a creak, there were more bloody prints in the hallway.

Thomas took in a great breath and held it as he made his way down the hall towards the kitchen. He could hear the radio playing softly. Someone was singing 'When I fall in love'. He could smell his mother's perfume it was strong as if the whole bottle had been spilled. The kitchen looked like a bomb had hit it. His mother wasn't much of a housekeeper and the house was usually untidy, but not like this. There was broken crockery and glassware everywhere and the radio, which was plugged in, was hanging by its wire from the socket on the wall, dangling down in front of the kitchen base unit. A large knife was sticking up from the table where it was embedded in the wood. The floor was sticky with blood a great pool of it spread from the sink to the door, in the middle of the pool lay the body of Thomas's mother. She was on her side with one arm outstretched as if she were trying to reach for the door. Her lips were twisted into a grimace, her eyes were wide open and her throat was sliced with a jagged cut from ear to ear. Clare's long brown hair was stuck to her head and to the floor with blood and her cotton housecoat was parted slightly to expose one blood-smeared breast.

Thomas felt his skinny legs give from under him, he sank to his knees and his mother's blood smeared his trousers and shoes. He could hear a terrible sound filling the room, a guttural, animal keening which reached a crescendo into a shrieking howl. Over and over the noise came, filling his ears and his mind with terror. Then he heard the voice in his head.

"It's all right, Son," it said. *"Everything will be all right. I'm with you now and I'll help you."*

He felt strong arms lift him from the floor and a policeman wrapped him in a blanket.

"Don't be frightened," the voice told him. *"Just go with the policeman. Someone else will sort out this mess. It's not your problem. Forget about it."*

"Thank you," he mouthed, but no sound came out.

The policeman gathered Thomas in his arms and carried him from the room. It was the last time he ever saw his mother and he cannot remember now how she looked before she was murdered. The voice in his head, the voice that helped him then, remains with him today guiding and instructing him, often bullying, it rules his every thought. Sometimes Thomas gets angry with it but he always obeys it.

The Coming of the Lord

Breaking the Thomas Malone case was an achievement but nothing could prepare DC Angela Murphy or her colleagues for the challenge ahead.

Escaped psychopathic sociopath John Baptiste, is big, powerful and totally out of control. Guided by his perverse religious interpretation of morality, he wreaks havoc.

An under-resourced police department struggles to cope, not only with this new threat, but also the ruthless antics of ganglord Jackie McGeachy.

Pressure mounts along with the body count.

Glasgow has never felt more dangerous.

Never Ever Leave Me

Katy Bradley had a perfect life, or so she thought. Perfect husband, perfect job and a perfect home until one day, one awful day when everything fell apart.

Full of fear and dread, Katy had no choice but to run, but would her split-second decision carry her forward to safety or back to the depths of despair? A chance encounter with a handsome stranger gives her hope.

Never ever leave me, sees Katy trapped between two worlds, her future and her past. Will she have the strength to survive? Will she ever find happiness again?

Death at Presley Park

In the center of a leafy suburb, everyone is having fun until the unthinkable happens. The man walks into the middle of the picnic ground seemingly unnoticed and without warning, opens fire indiscriminately into the startled crowd. People collapse, wounded and dying. Those who can, flee for their lives.

Who is this madman and why is he here? And when stakes are high, who will become a hero and who will abandon their friends?

Elly Grant's Death At Presley Park is a convincing psychological thriller.

But Billy Can't Fly

At over six feet tall, blonde and blue-eyed, Billy looks like an Adonis, but he is simple minded, not the full shilling, one slice less than a sandwich, not quite right in the head. When you meet him you might not notice at first, but after a couple of minutes it becomes apparent. The lights are on but nobody's home. In Billy's mind, he's Superman, a righter of wrongs, a saver of souls and that's where it all goes wrong. He interacts with the people he meets at a bus stop, Jez, a rich public schoolboy, Melanie the office slut, Bella Worthington, the leader of the local W.I. and David, a gay, Jewish teacher. This book moves quickly along as each character tells their part of the tale. Billy's story is darkly funny, poignant and tragic. Full of stereotypical prejudices, it offends on every level, but is difficult to put down.

Released by Elly Grant Together with Zach Abrams

Twists and Turns

With fear, horror, death and despair, these stories will surprise you, scare you and occasionally make you smile. *Twists and Turns* offer the reader thought provoking tales. Whether you have a minute to spare or an hour or more, open *Twists and Turns* for a world full of mystery, murder, revenge and intrigue.

A unique collaboration from the authors Elly Grant and Zach Abrams

Here's the index of Twists and Turns -

Table of Contents

A selection of stories by Elly Grant and Zach Abrams ranging in length across flash fiction (under 250 words), short (under 1000 words) medium (under 5000 words) and long (approx. 16,000 words)

and here's the first few pages to sample -

Waiting for Martha

The 'whoooo aaaaah' accompanied by blood curdling shrieks sent the Campbell brothers screaming down the path. They tore along the street without a backward glance. Martha Davis and her three companions doubled up with laughter. They were all dressed as zombies and, to the naïve eyes of primary school-aged children, they were the real thing.

"Did you see the middle one move?" Alan Edwards asked. "He could be a candidate for the Olympics. He easily left his big brother behind."

"That's because the older one's a lard ass," John Collins replied unkindly. "His bum cheeks wobbled like a jelly. Fat kids shouldn't wear lycra. If the real Superman was that chunky he'd never get off the ground."

"The middle one overtook him because he was trying to help the younger one and was holding his hand," Martha observed. "I'm sure that little fellow pee-ed his pants, he was terrified. He's only about five."

"Yeah, great isn't it?" Fiona Bell added laughing. "I love Halloween, don't you?" she said clapping her gloved hands together with pleasure.

The teenagers had hidden round the corner of Alan's house to jump out at unsuspecting children who came trick or treating. They were all aged fifteen except for John Collins whose birthday had been in June, he was sixteen but looked older. He was a big lad, tall and broad with an athletic build, he looked like a grown-up where the others still looked like children. Fiona Bell was nearly sixteen her birthday was on the fifth of November, Guy Fawkes night, so the group would be celebrating next week with fireworks. She was the spitting image of her mother being of medium height with long blonde hair and a heart shaped pretty face. Alan Edwards's birthday was in January. He was short with straggly black hair and he was a bit of a joker. Martha Davis, the baby of the group, was born in March and was a willowy looking beauty with Titian coloured hair. They were in the same class at school and had a reputation for being cool and edgy. None of them was ever actually caught for their various misdemeanours, but they were often seen running away from trouble. Being teenagers they thought they knew it all and, smoking, drinking, wearing only black and never telling their parents anything, was par for the course. Living in a village meant they didn't have easy access to drugs but the friends made roll-ups using everything from dried orange peel to crushed tree bark and convinced each other it had some psychedelic effect. They'd all been born in the village and had been friends since playgroup. They trusted one another with their worries and secrets and their friendships endured through petty squabbles and jealousies. Although unrelated, they were like a family.

By seven o'clock the procession of 'victims' had all but dried up, the word had got out, it seemed, so Martha and her friends decided to change venue.

"Time to go to church," Alan suggested. "If we hide just inside the gates of the churchyard, we'll get them as they walk by."

"That's a great idea," John added. "They'll think we've risen out of one of the churchyard graves. We'll scare the shit out of the little darlings."

"You lot go ahead and I'll catch you up. I'm going home for a warmer sweater and a quick bite to eat. I've not had my dinner yet and I'm starving. I'll just be about half an hour," Martha assured.

"Why didn't you grab something to eat before you came out? The rest of us did. Now you'll miss out on some of the fun," Fiona said, disappointedly. Martha was her best girl friend and she didn't want to be stuck on her own with the two boys. They could get incredibly silly without Martha. She was the mother figure of the group and she always managed to stop them from going too far.

"Don't worry Fiona, I'll not be long, and you two," she said pointing to the boys, "Behave yourselves."

"Yes Mom," they replied in unison, hanging their heads and pulling comical faces.

"See what I have to put up with when your not there, anyone would think they were two years old."

Martha stared at her three friends, her face had a serious expression and for a moment it looked as if she might cry. "I love you guys," she said. "I'll be as quick as I can."

"Are you okay?" Fiona asked. "You look a bit upset."

"I'm fine, really fine. My eyes are just watering with the cold. It's freezing out here."

Martha gave each of them a hug and off she raced towards her home. The others quickly made their way to the church and positioned themselves behind one of the large wrought iron gates. The gates hadn't been closed for over fifty years and ivy grew thickly round them affording the teenagers cover. For the next forty minutes they had a ball scaring adults and children alike until one of their teachers, Mr Johnston, came along. As the three friends jumped out shrieking he clutched his heart and fell to the ground. They thought they'd killed him. They were kneeling on the ground beside him each trying to decide how to do CPR when he suddenly sat up and shouted "Got ya." The tables were well and truly turned and they nearly jumped out of their skins.

"It's not so funny when you're on the receiving end is it?" he said rising to his feet. "Haven't you got homes to go to? And where's the fourth one? Where's your friend, Martha?"

"She went home for some food," Fiona said. "She should have been back by now."

"I think you should all run along and find her. You've done enough damage here for one night?"

Mr Johnston brushed himself down and walked away. After their shock the three friends had indeed had enough.

"Martha should have been here ages ago," Alan said. "I'm getting cold now. Let's go to her house and see what's keeping her."

"Good idea," John agreed.

"But what if she's on her way and we miss her?" Fiona protested.

"Come on," Alan said pulling her arm. "I'm not waiting any longer and you can't stay here on your own. A real zombie might leap out of a grave and get you. If Martha arrives and we're gone she'll go home and she'll find us there."

"I suppose you're right," Fiona conceded.

"I'm always right," Alan said smugly. "Come on let's get going before my ears fall off with the cold."

The three friends headed along the street towards Martha's home. They were damp and tired and they hoped that Helen Davis, Martha's mum, had hot soup for them. She always had soup on the stove in winter and she fed the three of them as if they were her family.

"I hope Mrs Davis has pumpkin soup, it's my favourite," John said,

"Yeah, the chilli she puts in it really gives it a kick," Alan agreed.

"Aren't either of you just a teensy bit worried about Martha? She's been gone for over an hour now and she's never usually late," Fiona said. "Get a move on, you two. I want to make sure she's all right."

When they reached Martha's house and rang the bell they were surprised when her Dad, Michael, answered instead of her.

"Well, well, what have we here?" he asked laughing at their attire. "Is Martha hiding? Where is she?"

"She left us over an hour ago to come home for food," Fiona said. "We thought she was still here. When did she leave the house?"

"Martha hasn't been home," her father replied. "If this is some sort of Halloween joke, it's not funny." He stared at the teenagers. "The joke's over. Where's Martha?"

A chill ran through each of the friends and Fiona's eyes welled with tears. "We don't know," she said helplessly. "If she didn't come home then she's been gone for over an hour. Something might have happened to her, maybe she's fallen. We'd better go back and look for her."

"Wait for me. I'm coming with you," Mr Davis replied. "I'll just go and tell Martha's mum what's happening."

After a couple of minutes, Michael Davis returned and Helen was with him. When she saw the state Fiona was in, Helen put her arm round the crying girl's shoulders and tried to reassure her. "Don't worry, Pet, we'll find her," she said. "She won't have gone far. She probably stopped to chat to someone and lost track of the time."

"We'll split into three groups," Michael Davis said. "Alan and John, you take the street leading to the church. Helen and Fiona, you walk towards the primary school and I'll take the road that goes round the outside of the village. We'll meet back here in half an hour. No, better make it forty-five minutes," he said looking at his watch.

The boys looked uncomfortably at Fiona; they would have much rather stayed together but they had no choice. Mr Davis had taken control and, as he was an adult and a teacher, they felt they should do what he said. Besides, the sooner they found Martha the sooner they could go home, assuming of course that they did find Martha.

They searched the whole village knocking on several doors as they went. The group met up after the arranged forty-five minutes then searched again. By ten o'clock there was nowhere left to look for her. The next day was a school day and the three teenagers had now reached their curfew, but they were reluctant to go home with Martha still missing. Michael Davis was grim faced. Helen was beginning to panic.

About the Author

Hi, my name is Elly Grant and I like to kill people. I use a variety of methods. Some I drop from a great height, others I drown, but I've nothing against suffocation, poisoning or simply battering a person to death. As long as it grabs my reader's attention, I'm satisfied.

I've written several novels and short stories. My first novel, 'Palm Trees in the Pyrenees' is set in a small town in France. It is published by Author Way Limited. Author Way has already published the next three novels in the series, 'Grass Grows in the Pyrenees,' 'Red Light in the Pyrenees' and 'Dead End in the Pyrenees' as well as a collaboration of short stories called 'Twists and Turns'.

As I live in a small French town in the Eastern Pyrenees, I get inspiration from the way of life and the colourful characters I come across. I don't have to search very hard to find things to write about and living in the most prolific wine producing region in France makes the task so much more delightful.

When I first arrived in this region I was lulled by the gentle pace of life, the friendliness of the people and the simple charm of the place. But dig below the surface and, like people and places the world over, the truth begins to emerge. Petty squabbles, prejudice, jealousy and greed are all there waiting to be discovered. Oh, and what joy in that discovery. So, as I sit in a café, or stroll by the riverside, or walk high into the mountains in the sunshine I greet everyone I meet with a smile and a 'Bonjour' and, being a friendly place, they return the greeting. I people watch as I sip my wine or when I go to buy my baguette. I discover quirkiness and quaintness around every corner. I try to imagine whether the subjects of my scrutiny are nice or nasty and, once I've decided, some of those unsuspecting people, a very select few, I kill.

Perhaps you will visit my town one day. Perhaps you will sit near me in a café or return my smile as I walk past you in the street. Perhaps you will hold my interest for a while, and maybe, just maybe, you will be my next victim. But don't concern yourself too much, because, at least for the time being, I always manage to confine my murderous ways to paper.

Read books from the 'Death in the Pyrenees' series, enter my small French town and meet some of the people who live there – and die there.

To contact the author email to ellygrant@authorway.net

To purchase books by Elly Grant link to http://author.to/ellygrant

Lightning Source UK Ltd.
Milton Keynes UK
UKHW022055170821
389030UK00009B/555/J